Two Dramatic Poems:

THE ANGEL OF SUFFERING

ZEAMI

A Bilingual Edition in English and Japanese

守口三郎　英日詩集

劇詩　受難の天使　世阿弥

Saburo Moriguchi

Translated by Naoshi Koriyama
Edited by Bruce Allen

Coal Sack Publishing Company
コールサック社

Two Dramatic Poems:

THE ANGEL OF SUFFERING
ZEAMI

劇詩　受難の天使　世阿弥

CONTENTS

Translator's Introduction

When I first read this book of two dramatic poems, "The Angel of Suffering" and "Zeami," I was deeply impressed by the author's profound knowledge of many fields and by his admirable literary power. The author, the late Prof. Saburo Moriguchi, consulted the Old and New Testaments, books on theology, philosophy, history, anthropology, geography, as well as research works and papers concerning Caucasia. For the second poem, "Zeami," he widely consulted various sacred writings of Buddhism, sayings of Zen, sermons of Buddhist priests, Noh plays, essays and talks on Noh by Zeami, and research books on Zeami. He also consulted the *Dictionary of the Japanese Language in the Muromachi Period* and the *Dictionary of Sado Dialect*.

This book is based on the author's wide and deep learnings in many fields. His thoughts and feelings are expressed vividly and beautifully.

The speech of the Helping Angel in Act V of the first poem, well describes the evolution of human beings, from their lives in the trees to their lives on the ground, walking on two legs. Advances in their skills of obtaining food and property, as well as the serious problems caused by their insatiable greed, are well described, as in the following passages:

"People learned the techniques of farming and stock-raising.
    And thus, their living became stable and they increased their descendants.
    But human beings strengthened their senses of self-preservation
    Far beyond their instincts for living. And their Greed grew ever larger,
    And finally, out of the Muddy Sea of Whirling Desires,
    A Demoniac Poison Snake of Greed leaped up.....

"When they owned and saved things beyond their needs,
    They feared plunder by other tribes, built fortresses and armed themselves.
    Fear bred Distrust, Distrust bred Hostility,
    Hostility induced Attacks. Fear is the Mother of Wickedness....."

Then, the Angel of Justice says:

"People basking in the morning Sun may change their cold, fossil-like hearts
Into warm hearts of blood and flesh.
They may get off the Vehicle of Destruction,
Step onto the ground of the Dawning World,
Feeling its texture underfoot again, and slowly start walking.

"They will stop and stand, healing the wounds of the Earth
        with their tears and sweat,
Healing the diseases of the Earth with Compassion and Care.
They will transform deserts into green fields, praise the revived flowers,
Listen to the songs of the birds that have returned,
And harvest the crops, the gifts of the Earth."

I think this dramatic poem, "The Angel of Suffering," is one of the most important dramatic poems ever written; so vividly, so powerfully and so beautifully.

The second poem, "Zeami," mainly consists of dialogues between an unemployed contemporary Japanese man travelling on Sado Island and the ghost of Zeami (1363-1443), who was a player and writer of Noh and a critic. The ghost of Zeami says to the traveler in Act III:

"On a beautiful spring day I went to the seaside, stood by the rocky seashore
Upon which white waves were sweeping, and looking over the rapid current
        full of fishes,
I danced to the roaring sounds of the Sea, considering them the chantings
        of the Dragon God,
Dancing to the drum of the furious waves beating on the rocks,
Looking toward the Light shining brightly from the end of the Sea,
Dedicating my dance to the gods and Buddha who mercifully give us groupers,

Praying for safe fishing in the Sea, praying for calming down the winds

"When clouds of cherry blossoms covered distant mountains,
I was tempted by the cherry blossoms, and quickly set out with a merry heart,
In the bright cherry blossoms falling and fluttering in the wind
And enjoyed looking at the wild flowers blooming and falling in the fields,
But I realized that the image of the Flower of Light appearing in each
      and every heart
Is none other than the Eternal, Immortal Flower.
And I turned into the spirit of cherry blossoms in the Sky, and I danced
To the flute music of the stormy winds going over the mountains,
Blowing down the cherry blossoms, the dances of "Peace in Transience,"
"Joy in Transformation," and "Flowers scattering in Buddha's World,"
      not knowing whither I was going,

"Assuming that it might be my last chance to savor the departing spring,
I went out to the fields where flowers were abundantly blooming
In the gentle winds to talk with the flowers of various colors,
And when I got into the woods of green young leaves lit in the Sun,
I danced at the fresh-aired shrine to the flutes and drums of the mountain birds
Which were freely singing, and to the chanting of the loud sound of the stream.
I stood by planted rice paddies in gentle breezes, praying for a rich crop
      of golden rice.
I danced to the loud chanting of the frogs in the distant paddies
      as far as Heaven
In praise of all the green mountains as far as I could see."

I realize that no words of my Introduction can adequately explain the beauty, the power and the excellence, of these two dramatic poems by the late Prof. Saburo Moriguchi. I will just let the poems speak for themselves. It was a great experience for me to translate these two great dramatic poems into English. I hope many people, young and old, all over the world will enjoy reading this book. I extend my deep gratitude to Mrs. Saburo Moriguchi and Hisao Suzuki, president of Coal Sack Publishing Company, for their generous assistance in bringing out this English translation to people the world over.

I would also like to extend my hearty gratitude to Prof. Bruce Allen for editing my English translation. I would also like to thank the librarians of Sagamihara City Library for helping me with questions about Zeami. Finally I would like to ask the readers to note that I took the liberty to capitalize the first letter of some of the nouns and adjectives in my attempt to emphasize their importance. For example:

"Fear bred Distrust, Distrust bred Hostility,
  Hostility induced Attacks. Fear is the Mother of Wickedness..."

Naoshi Koriyama
Poet, and professor emeritus at Toyo University
November 2019

I

A Dramatic Poem: *THE ANGEL OF SUFFERING*

Characters: Traveling Monk
             Local Old Man
             Helping Angel
             Angel of Justice

Location: In the Mountain of Southern Caucasia

Time: Early winter of a year toward the end of the 12th Century

Act I A Mountain Pass Leading to a Ridge

(A young monk in a traveling outfit, carrying a bag on his back,
holding a stick in his hand appears on a mountain pass.)

TRAVELING MONK

How fast the winter days pass by! It was in May, more than half a year ago
That I set out from the woods in the North, in a season
When everything was in fresh green, and the birds in the woods
Were singing in praise of my departure on a pilgrimage.
Since then, I made my way, walking across the great prairies
Where the scorching sun was beating on the ground,
Strong winds were raging in summer, and I passed through the plains
Where rolling waves of golden grains were swaying in autumn,
And I crossed the dead winter fields covered with white frost,
On which winter winds were howling loud,
And I managed to go over the steep Caucasian highlands with the caravan,
And further going over the plains by myself, and gasping, I struggled
Going along the mountain trail leading to the ridges.
It's all because I am planning to visit the Church in Jerusalem
And start a new life as a monk.
However, like the changes of seasons, the end of one's life comes quickly.
Many people in ancient times died on the roads.
Even if my ambitious spirit is anxious to realize its aspiration, the goal is far.
To live each day of my life fully is the right way.
Oh, the dark closes in on me, and snow has begun to fall,
Preventing me from moving forward.
Keeping on going blindly where I no longer can see anything is a reckless,
     foolish act,
It's not a brave act at all. Even if I am ready to die on the road,

Dying, freezing on the road vainly is not a right way.
Now, I should find the shade of a rock and pass the severe cold winter night
      on the mountain.

(*An old man carrying a grass basket appears in front of him.*)

LOCAL OLD MAN

Ah, traveling man, there, where are you going at this hour of nightfall?

TRAVELING MONK

This mountain trail has been unexpectedly steep, the sun set
      before I crossed over the ridge,
And even snow has begun to fall. I am looking for a cave or the shade
Of a rock, where I can shelter myself for the night.

LOCAL OLD MAN

It's reckless of you. Your body may not be able to endure the severe cold
Of the night in the snowing mountain.
Moreover, this is a dangerous place where wolves prowl about
      in the dark of night.
I just finished my day's work, and I'm on my way to my hut nearby.
Please come with me. It's a small, crude, humble hut in the valley,
But it should be good enough for you to spend the cold night.

TRAVELING MONK

It's so kind of you. (*Aside*) The help given by this old man must be the work
Of my guardian Angel. Truly, Almighty God tenderly treats even tiny creatures
On Earth, paying kind attention. How indescribably precious is divine Providence!

All that I can offer is a humble prayer.
May God's will be done in everything!

Act II   Hut in the Valley

(*The old man leads the monk to the hut in the woods of the valley.*)

LOCAL OLD MAN

This log hut is a simple shelter with only two rooms,
But it is shaded from strong sunshine and can stop violent winds.
I found this spot where a mountain stream flows
And I began to build a temporary lodge for hunting forty years ago.
I kept reinforcing it. I added a storehouse.
The hut has become as old as this old body of mine, but it's still livable.
The sun has set and it's dark, so let me put a light on.

(*The old man takes a flint and a piece of iron out of a box,
and using them, he strikes a spark, which he moves to tinder and then,
to the dish of oil, and then, he kindles sticks in the hearth on the floor.*)

Now, Traveler, please come closer and warm your body with the fire.
Please make yourself at home. And I'll get supper ready.

(*He puts some dried mutton and vegetables into the pot hanging
on the adjustable hook above the fireplace and boils it.*)

In this valley, the stream moistens the earth. And fog rises and hangs,
And the sun shines moderately.
Consequently, edible wild plants and mushrooms
Are plentiful, and we get plenty of vegetables on the farm.
In autumn, colorful fruit woods are full of fruits such as pears, walnuts,
        chestnuts, plums, and grapes.
Here, in our place, as long as we plant and grow vegetables,
Pick up mushrooms and fruits and put them in the storeroom,

We don't run out of food even in the winter
When the life of everything decays and hides in the ground.
Vegetables on the farm, sheep in the pasture, nuts and animals in the woods,
Yes, everything is the grace given by the Earth, the gift from God.
People in the mountains live, feeding on the lives of these things.
The fat of mutton is the oil of this lamp, shining in the dark of night.
Therefore, my solitary life in the mountain is free from want.

(*The old man puts the cooked food in a dish, and pours wine
out of a jar into cups.*)

Now, this is just simple food cooked in a pot. Please help yourself.
But first, let's make a toast with the wine.
It is said that this district was started
By Noah and his family who came out of the Ark
Which had finally run aground on the summit of Mt. Ararat,
When the flood of the ancient times had retreated
After covering the entire surface of the Earth.
They began to grow grapes on the fertile land over which a rainbow was hanging,
And made wine and got drunk.
This is a country that is famous for its wine.
The local people all enjoy making wine by themselves.

TRAVELING MONK

What a happy life you have here, enjoying your self-sufficient way of life!
Like sacred hermits of ancient times who lived out their life
        in the hottest deserts,
Or in steep craggy mountains, or on solitary islands in the raging sea,
You searched for a hermit-like way of life in this remote mountain, didn't you?

LOCAL OLD MAN

No, I am not a hermit. When I was young, I lived as a hunter in the village.
I was blessed with a good wife, but she passed away,
And when I was left a widower,
I just moved to the mountain, where it was convenient to live as a hunter.
Now, I cultivate a small, sunny, empty patch, and grow some vegetables
    and herbs.
From time to time, I go down the mountain to sell my herbs at the drugstore
In the village, buy some mutton in the market and come back.
After doing business in the village, I enjoy drinking tea with the merchants.
As I hear news about countries far, I can see the situation
    of the world very well.
I have never been away from this mountain area, but as for you, a young man,
Whence do you come and whither do you go? And I see you speak
The Armenian language of this area, but you seem to be a traveler
From a foreign country, not a native young man of this mountain area.

TRAVELING MONK

I have come from a northern country faraway, planning
    to visit the Holy Land of Jerusalem.
The principality of Kiev had been split into more than ten little parts
As a result of inner conflicts, the country has become chaotic,
Even the monastery in the woods far away from villages was plundered,
And it was closed, some Brothers returning to their homes,
And others moving to the north, each scattering in every direction.
As I had no relatives, I went to a town on the Volga River and worked
For about two years for an Armenian merchant who was trading there
With northern countries. During that time, I learned the Armenian language
And I got information about the roads and towns leading
    to the Anatolian area from Caucasia

And further I could learn about the caravans.

Thus, I made preparations for my pilgrimage to the Holy Land.

Finally, I sailed down the Volga River this spring, working on a pasture

In summer, and helping people harvest on the farm in autumn.

In the town of Shemakha, I was hired as a handy man by the caravan

Which was going westward, and I went along the trade route
      with the merchants,

Looking up at the great Caucasian range of white, snow-covered
      high mountains on the right,

And there, at the town of Tiflis, I left the caravan which was going
      to Trebizond.

Then I walked my own way alone, staying at local monasteries
      in each district,

And going over the mountains of South Caucasia, I came.

From there on, passing through Ani, Bitlis, and Edessa, and then, from Aleppo

I intend to go southward along the way to the Holy Land of Jerusalem.

There in the Holy Land, I'd like to work, repairing churches
      and helping the pilgrims.

Then I plan to enter the monastery on the steep Mt. Carmel,

Where monks are said to have lived in seclusion since ancient times,

Or if I can't follow my intended plans, I'd like to go to Greece

By sea and enter the monastery on the Holy Mt. Athos.

I have studied Greek steadily at the monastery in the North Country,

Which I hope will be of some use.

LOCAL OLD MAN

(*Aside*) How beautiful this young man looks, who bravely lives
with a right goal in his heart! The young man is a rising sun shining
bright with a clear light. The young man's beautiful image is a floral
crown of life, which only he is blessed to wear. Thoughtfulness often
joins hands with Fear, creeping into the bed of Indolence. The Thought-

fulness of a brave young man joins hands with Enthusiasm,
working actively, conquering any kind of difficulties. This power is
     none other than the pride of the young man.
(*To the monk*) Only by virtue of your wisdom and courage,
You may be able to make your way on the long, dangerous travel.
But the road of pilgrimage seems to be filled with even more risks than before.
So please be careful along the way.
Huge hosts of fanatic militias wearing the cross insignia on their bodies came,
Invading from the west a hundred years ago, repeating mass slaughters
And plundering in Antioch and the Capital City of Jerusalem,
And after chasing away the local residents from Syria and Palestine,
They took the land. With all these acts, feelings of Hatred
Against the invading Christians were spawned in the hearts
Of the Muslims who had been originally tolerant toward people
     of other religions,
And it is only natural that Hatred has taken deep roots after many years.
I hear that peace was made recently and a truce has been arranged
And safe trips to the Holy Land are assured, but the peace will not
     be kept for long.
The temporary peace is the result of the clever handling of the times
     by the conflicting kings.
Powerful persons, blinded by Greed, will easily rip the patched fabric
Of apparent Peace, and peaceful kingdoms will be destroyed
By an invading powerful empire, and the great empire itself too
Will finally perish due to inner disruptions, revolts of its dependent territories,
Or invasions by other foreign peoples, toward the end of their fate,
Thus exposing only the ruins of their prosperous dreams.
It is just as it is said: "All they that take the sword shall perish with the sword."
Truly, Peace of the World is a delicate balance in time
Which is in constant, rolling motion. It is just a temporary harmony
     appearing out of the ceaselessly changing chaos.
In order to keep the constantly moving Peace as long as possible,

We need fresh Wisdom and Agility of a youthful Spirit.

TRAVELING MONK

As Caucasia is a mountainous region with a range of lofty peaks,
Foreign people's greed will be kept away, and the people here in the mountains
Will be able to lead a peaceful life without worries for a long time.

LOCAL OLD MAN

No matter how steep the mountains may be, the limitless, sky-high Greed
Of kings can't be discouraged. Wandering minstrels of this area tell us
That many kingdoms ruled Caucasia and perished,
Because Caucasia is situated at the cultural crossroads.
Various tribes looked for fertile lands, settled down in livable flat lands
        or valleys since ancient times.
Though there were some conflicts and troubles at the beginning,
They learned the Wisdom for living together as time passed by,
And they have found a way to live together peacefully. And now,
Village people from different tribes associate with each other closely,
Enjoying themselves at the same banquet tables,
Attending each other's weddings and funerals.
People, whether they are Christians, Muslims or people belonging
To some other religions, recognize each other's religion,
And they respect each other's sacred place.
But, should the big countries in the north and south of Caucasia wish
To expand their territories by force and fight,
This peaceful mountain region could turn into a front-line battleground,
Causing the villagers great suffering.
If the ruler of the empire ruling this area should turn out to be despotic,
He may divide this area willfully, slaughtering any resisting mountain people,
And bring his own people here and let them live here,

Expelling the members of other religions. The smoldering grudges
Of the mistreated people caused by the suffering would flame up
As a flame of Hatred, and keep the conflicts among different peoples
Through later ages, staining these clean mountain areas red with blood,
And the murky Malice would curse the old enemy, and keep cursing the past.
This kind of misery too is the result of human nature.
Hurts in the hearts caused by the conflicts will keep afflicting the people
For a long time, and a period of three peaceful generations won't be
　　　long enough to heal the hearts.

Well, my talk is endless, but please take a good rest in the next room
　　　after you drink some tea,
Because you have to set out early tomorrow morning.
Fortunately, the snow that was falling has now stopped.
It will be fine tomorrow. Even so, the mountain trail over the ridge
And down to the foot of the mountain is long. You had better set out
Early tomorrow morning with plenty of time on your hands.
You should walk up the byway from this hut, return
To the original mountain trail and aim for the ridge.
That's the safest way. I won't see you off or guide you tomorrow morning.
Please forgive my lack of attention. For some reason, I have to set out
Before the sky grows white at dawn tomorrow to go to a certain place
And perform a certain service, which is done once every ten days.
Even if you happen to see me on the mountain, please keep away from me.
It will be enough if you add a prayer for my peace of mind to your prayers.
That's all that I ask you.
I'll get your breakfast for tomorrow and prepare some ready-to-eat food
　　　for two days ready for you.
Put some water from this bottle into your water bottle.
Don't leave any recompense for me. You keep your humble travel expenses
　　　for your further travel.
We people of this area are proud of ourselves helping our guests.

When you leave tomorrow morning, please bolt the door from outside,
So that no animals may get into the hut. I sincerely wish you
A safe journey, starting tomorrow. So, take a good rest. And good night!

TRAVELING MONK

Thank you for the food and space to sleep which you provided for me tonight.
And I just can't thank you enough for the food you've prepared for me
        for a few more days from tomorrow.
And the talks you've given me will be food for my heart.
All your kindness is a blessing from merciful God.
I will never forget this once-in-a-lifetime grace in all my life.
You say you will set out early tomorrow morning for some reason.
May God bless you with abundant grace! I wish you good health
        and happiness forever.
Please excuse me. Good night.

Act III   A Trail near the Summit of the Mountain

TRAVELING MONK

(*Aside*) Oh, how gracious God is! The morning sun shines, and the snow melts.
My feet lightly bound, as I go along the mountain trail,
Where a white fog is clearing up.
In the clean air, my heart is clear and I feel refreshed.
How blessed I am as I go along the mountain trail in the gentle light!
The kind old man's hospitality has relieved me of my fatigue,
And I'm blessed with fine weather this morning.
My journey along the mountain trail today will go smoothly,
And I may be able to go over the ridge in the morning.

From the roundabout route all around this high rocky mountain
A narrower trail leading to the summit of the mountain branches off.
What shall I do? It would be safe to keep going along this mountain trail
    like this.
But, if I take the narrower trail, I may be able to get a wider view
And see the panoramic view of this area as well. If the mountain tail is
    too rugged,
I can just give up and return. The weather is fine and it's early in the morning,
So I will take this narrower trail.

This is a rocky spot not far from the summit. I can see the range
Of the mountains of Caucasia over which I have crossed, highlands,
Pastures, the river glistening white, and I can see the dark forests
    and deep gorges just below my eyes.
The great space of this world is filled with bright light,
And everything is peacefully wrapped in tranquility.

Oh, I can hear a faint sound. Is it the sound of a falling rock?

Or is it the cry of some animal in the woods brought by the wind?
No, it's a sound coming from a closer place.
It's coming from the front.
Is it the sound of a wind cutting the edge of a rock?
Is it the cry of a goat climbing up a rock wall? Or is it a call of an eagle
hiding in a rocky cave?
I can see a cave by the roadside ahead. The sound seems to be coming
from that rock cave over there.

(*The monk goes closer to the cave and looks in.*)

Something is moving in the inner part of the dark cave into which no light
is shining.
Is it a bird? An animal? Ah, it's a human being lying down there, groaning.

Act IV   A Cave in the Rocky Place

(*The monk goes closer to the human being lying in the inner part of the cave and stoops down.*)

TRAVELING MONK

Hello, what is the matter? Oh, what a terrible thing! This is the old man
Who helped me last night! Hello! Can you see me?

LOCAL OLD MAN

Ah, a dark figure is coming closer to me, when I am being burned
    in the Hell fire.
Who are you? My body is being burned into fragments in torture by fire,
Tears in my eyes have dried up, my eyes are hazy, and I can't even see the things
    right in front of my eyes.
Ah, a ghost holds my hands! Are you an executioner
Coming from the rugged, spear-like mountains of Hell?
Or are you an envoy from the Nether World, who has come to take me?
Where will you take me? If you can save me from the living fire of Hell,
You may take me anywhere. Now, take me out of here quick!
Pray, take me to the painless Nether World, and sink me
    into the calm dark.
I'd like to dissolve into the void of Eternal Nirvana.
Well, the voice speaking into my ear sounds familiar.....
Do you want to take me back to the World?
If you are a villager, don't come into the grave and prevent me from setting out
On a journey to the Nether World.
What are you going to do with me rolling around in the fire?
Oh, this is the Traveling Monk! How did you ever come here? I told you
Not to come closer to me in the mountain. I need no care. You don't have

To give me any water from your bottle.

Keep the water that you will need for your mountain journey.

Just leave me alone. I just want to hide this miserable image of mine
from others.

This is a painful affliction that has been plaguing me once in ten days
since some time ago.

Even our village doctor doesn't know anything about it.

I grew some herb and used it, but no medicine could heal this disease.

The older I get, the more painful it gets.

My mind gets confused, my senses get foggy, and the end of my life can come
any minute.

Even if I breathe my last here, you don't have to go back to the village and tell
the villagers about it.

This cave is my secret grave. I am ready to die and turn into dust.

Now, don't care about me, who am like a dead body.

Make haste and go over the mountain.

TRAVELING MONK

(*Aside*) I cannot help this person who is suffering from severe pain.

Attending a suffering person can be a nuisance to him sometimes.

What should I do? I am powerless. All that I can do now for the old man is
just pray. I will pray for God's mercy,

So that this person may be relieved of his pains and have peace.

(*The Monk goes out of the cave.*)

LOCAL OLD MAN

Ah, Ouch! Ouch! Ouch!

A poisonous snake, constricting my whole body, bites and tears me up
with its fangs,

A throng of creeping worms attack me with their poisonous stings,
Thus spoiling and devouring my muscles.
With these all-out attacks from my enemies,
My body's citadel is destroyed, and my mind's headquarters is smashed.
My body and mind are broken into pieces, still burning up,
Coloring Heaven and Earth in red!
You, burnt up body, and you, melted brains, don't cling to this place,
Burn up yourselves and go away somewhere!
Has the executioner from Hell gone away, terrified by this living Hell?
Where is the messenger from the Nether World?
Is he coldly looking at this painful reality from some distance?
Envoy of Death, come quickly!
Cut off this burnt brand of life
With your big shears completely!
......The sight of my eyes has darkened.
I should be able to leave for the Nether World at last, shouldn't I?

Where am I? Where am I in this dark space?
Have I gone into the Nether World now?
As I am conscious and my mind is working,
I may not be dead, it seems. Have I been sent back to this world?
Was my mind so confused because of the too great pains?
And did it make me blurt out crazy things, pleading for death?
When the storm of severe pains passes by, my consciousness,
After flying around in the maddened, rough space, regains clarity,
Returning to its nest of sanity under the clear Sky.
I am in the cave. I am still lying down
In the rock cave as before.

I have been crying out from the tormenting flames,
But God has remained silent, not answering me.
I have pleaded from the bottom of my suffering,

But the Lord doesn't answer, remaining silent in the dark.
Is this place Purgatory that burns out earthly Desires?
Not the eternal Hell?

Ah, how gracious! Cool water drops come oozing out from the rock ceiling!
When I receive the water drops with my burning tongue, my thirst is quenched.
When I moisten my scorching body with these water drops,
The burning pain is relieved.
This is none other than the sacred water given by God.
Are these cool water drops the answer from the Lord?
Doesn't the Lord still want to burn and destroy my body,
Telling me to cool it with water?

Oh, cleansed with the clean water soaking through my body,
I seem to have regained my calm senses and have returned to the world of light
    from the entrance of the Nether World!
If I have jumped around in the torrid heat of the flames, have lost my
    consciousness,
Have been taken by the Devil, and have blurted out numerous, dirty, sinful words,
Please, Lord, forgive this miserable me!
I believe that the Lord will not forsake me,
And leading me with His Compassion, will save me.

Act V A Roadside in the Rocky Mountain

(*The Traveling Monk is praying by the roadside at a bend in the road outside the cave.*)

TRAVELING MONK

(*Aside*) What light is that? The light is lighting up even the back
    of my closed eyes?
The sky I am looking at is the same blue sky, as usual. The view is
    the same as usual.
But, why, I wonder, is only this area unusually bright?
Ah, the rocky wall near the top of the mountain above the cave is shining.
Ah, a huge image like that of a human figure is clinging to the rock wall, shining.
No, it's not clinging to the rock of its own will, but its hands and feet are
Bound to the sharp edge of the rock by a shaft of blinding light.
What is that shining image? Has the ghost of Prometheus, who was bound
To the rocky mountain of Caucasia in Greek mythology appeared?
Or, is it the Archangel who insolently considered himself
As great as God and was expelled from the Heavens
And is kept hanging on this rocky mountain?

HELPING ANGEL

Who is it speaking to me that have come down to this land?
The people of these mountain areas have been praising me
And singing of me as Amirani, the child of the Sun,
A hero of Resistance who was punished by the God and bound
To the rocky mountain for bringing the fire to human beings,
And the people of Greece have been praising me as demi-God,
Prometheus, who led human beings defying the chief God
And thus have been handing down the story of my suffering.

But I am neither Amirani nor Prometheus who was punished
By the God, nor am I the Angel who opposed the God and was expelled.
I am the Angel who has attended human beings for the purpose
Of helping them develop their minds.

TRAVELING MONK

Ah, how mysterious it is! If you are such a Holy Angel, how can the Angel
Of pure spirit appear in the image of a human being? And also,
Why is the Holy Angel helping human beings develop their minds bound
    on the rocky wall?

HELPING ANGEL

Your question is understandable, but a purely spiritual Angel isn't
    necessarily invisible.
The true nature of an Angel is the power of spirit, and the power
    of an Angel can also work
In a human figure, since an Angel is a spirit.
Just look at the charitable people working in the World.
And also, look at those saints who have become models for human beings.
When a human being earnestly prays for an Angel's help,
The Helping Angel instantly appears in the person's mind and helps.
An Angel may sometimes take the form of a human being,
    depending on the needs.
There is some special reason why I have appeared in a human figure
And in the strange form crucified
On this rocky mountainside. Now, let me tell you about the reason.

Ever since the Lord decided to create human beings,
Selected their ancestors from among the primates, and blew the factor
Of the human spirit into them, I have been sent to the Earth from Heaven

On a mission to develop the minds of human beings,
I have accompanied them on the trees, carefully observing the development
of their minds.
As the climate of the land became drier, forests decreased and grasslands increased,
And the most ancient human beings came down from the trees, went out
over grasslands.
In order to protect themselves, they learned to stand up erect with their hind legs,
To look over their wide surroundings, and to walk and run with their two legs.
Valuing the function of the group which saved their lives, they learned
To develop their abilities in it.
They transformed their free forelegs into hands, dug up root crops with sticks,
Broke hard fruit coats, cut up the meat of small animals or dead animals
With a piece of stone, and ate it.
Look! Human beings put their large skulls and brains on their long legs,
Rich buttocks, broad pelvis, supple spines, and equipped
with rich networks of nerves,
They have stood up on the ground, used their brains and skillful hands,
And expanded their world with my help.
They have processed wood, stone, and bones and horns of animals,
And made various tools and improved them.
They gathered plants, hunted animals, and moved around in search of food.
They shared their scant food with other members of their group
With a sense of Compassion and unconscious Wisdom.
Primitive men, with their developed Intelligence, urged by strong Curiosity,
Bravely approached the embers of the fires in the woods started by lightning,
Or the lava flows that had gushed out of craters and hardened,
And they transferred the mysterious fire to firewood, and carried it
To their dwellings, the rock caves.
They never let the fire die out, and lit the dark with the fire,
and warmed their freezing bodies.
The flames of fire kept the hungry animals away, the animals clattering their fangs.
Instead, they chased their preys into pits or down cliffs

With torches in their hands. They broiled the cut meat of animals,
Boiled hard plants till they became soft, and enjoyed them.
The sacred fire in the rock cave gave them peace of mind,
Strengthening the warm, affectionate bond among family members.

At last, primitive men, using their Intelligence, rubbed the pointed tips of sticks
Or pieces of stone and struck sparks, which they transferred to dried grasses
Or animal fat, and thus tamed the God-given fire.
After getting hold of the precious fire of light and heat in their hands,
They boldly hunted for preys and stepped into unknown grounds,
Steep highlands, and even into plains in the north. In the glacial age,
They wore animal furs, made fires, and kept the fire of life in caves
        and temporary huts.
Protected by the fire, a man and a woman made love in the flame of Love
And hugged the new-born fruit of their Love with much affection.
The baby returned its smiles to its smiling mother,
And the exchange of Love became the root of the soul,
        nourishing the infant's mind.
The father taught his son how to make stoneware and hunt;
The mother taught her daughter how to pick edible plants
        and weave decorative articles.
In order to impart the skills for living and knowledge among themselves correctly,
Human beings invented Language and spoke to their children repeatedly.
Through actions and Language, they learned skills and knowledge and developed.
Language defined the uses of things and also showed the relationship
Between one thing and the other.
A genuine word uttered out of deep silence carried great weight,
Giving the light of existence to the depth of the listener's soul,
And stimulated and cultivated his Intelligence.
As a result, the feelings of human beings became richer, and their Intelligence
        more advanced.
They mourned the death of someone they loved, prayed for the person's

life in the Next World,
Adorned the dead body with flowers, buried it together with some articles
        in the grave.
And they revered the noble animals which were killed
By coming close to the hunters' group, and gave them their meat,
And supported human lives.
The animals were filled with power, beauty and dignity,
And the people painted the sacred animals whose lives were sacrificed,
Coloring them in the crimson of their life blood
On the inner rock walls of the caves, praising and worshiping their divine nature.
Human beings heard the Lord's voice in the sound of a wind and thunder,
Saw the eyes of God in the daytime and night,
In the Sun and the Moon. They played with flowers, dancing in the fields,
Bathed in the streams, took a nap, exposing their naked bodies to the Sun.
When hungry, they looked for animals and plants, moving to the woods rich
        in foods.
Being innocent, they were blessed with what the Lord and Nature gave them,
And they were in harmony with all things in the Universe, living in peace.
I have been blessing the World of human beings living in harmony,
        looking after their primeval Paradise.

TRAVELING MONK

I can understand that ever since human beings were created,
They passed through long primitive ages,
Created culture, adapting themselves to the harsh environment,
Enhancing their Intelligence, guided by the Angels sent by God,
Enriching their feelings, and developing their minds.
If so, why did the human beings who had been placed in the Garden
        as told in the Bible
Ever start hating each other and killing each other?
And why were they driven out of the Garden of Supreme Bliss?

HELPING ANGEL

Its fundamental reason is a mystery beyond human understanding.
God's Thought is far beyond the Intelligence of the Angels
     who were created by God.
All that human beings can know is nothing but the state of Evil.
In order to keep away from Evil that attracts them,
They must know the true state of Evil correctly: this is their duty.

Human beings have cultivated their God-given minds, and freely using their power,
They expanded the areas of their living. Women cultivated a kind of wild grass,
And succeeded to make wheat out of it by improving it.
People learned the techniques of farming and stock-raising.
And thus, their living became stable and they increased their descendants.
But human beings strengthened their sense of self-preservation
Far beyond their instincts for living. And their Greed grew ever larger,
And finally, out of the Muddy Sea of Whirling Desires,
A Demoniac Poison Snake of Greed leaped up.
The settled people used their Imagination, and made preparations
     for the uncertain Future.
For safety, they came to own land, saved foods and domestic animals.
Property increased their Fear, Fear increased their Property.
When they owned and saved things beyond their needs,
They feared plunder by other tribes, built fortresses and armed themselves.
Fear bred Distrust, Distrust bred Hostility,
Hostility induced Attack. Fear is the Mother of Wickedness.
Driven by Anxiety, holding on to blind Hope, human beings strove
To find fertile land moistened by a big river and settled there,
Specialized their work, efficiently accumulated Properties,
And built cities fortified with encircling walls.
Soon a strong man became a King, who organized an Army,

Attacked other cities, grabbed properties, owned slaves for labor.

In this way, human beings strengthened their Aggressiveness toward each other,

Thus, they were always threatened by War. Evil increased

Not only in civilized society, but also Crimes increased among individual persons.

Human beings looked for worldly Wealth with all their minds,

Gathered in cities, seeking Pleasure and Prosperity, worshiping the Idol of Gold,

But all they got was the material gods of this World.

And their mind's inclining toward Wickedness never stopped.

It was all because their Arrogance which looked for Independence rebelled
against the true God,

Hid at the bottom of their hearts, and concealed various Crimes.

The Arrogance that was born at full term gave birth to Vanity,

A Desire for Fame, Conceit, Egotism, and a Cold Heart.

Jealousy gave birth to Malice, Lie, Hatred, and Curses.

Mistaken Anger gave birth to Discord, Insult, Violence, Killing, Injuring,
and Resentment.

Greed, working with Egotism, bred a Desire for Wealth,
a Desire for Domination, and Voracity.

Carnal Desire degraded to Promiscuity and Adultery.

The Indolence of their hearts led human beings to lose Moderation,

Making them indulge in the mire of Pleasures.

These Wrongdoings, looking for chances, worked together in secret,

And gave birth to one Crime after another.

God, pitying the miserable plight of human beings who had sunk
to the depth of Wickedness,

Took the form of a human being, and appeared on the Earth,

Showing them the way to Salvation from Sins and Death.

Since early times, the Lord also gave a new mission to me,

An Angel who is helping human beings develop their minds.

Day after day I am bound to the rocky mountain,

And I keep redeeming the Evil of Arrogance that lies deep

in the roots of human hearts.

The Sins of human beings were definitely redeemed

By the Suffering of Jesus Christ, the Son of God,

And the Love of God forgave human beings and allowed them to live.

And the redemption by the Angel is doing a part of the sacred work of Christ,
    the Redeemer.

Therefore, I, who am with human beings, appear in the form of a man,

Am bound to the rocky wall every day, struck by God's Justice, even from now on.

Look! How would the Angel of Justice appear from Heaven
    and what would he do to me!

TRAVELING MONK

(*Aside*) Ah, A Great Pure-White Eagle has appeared out of the shining clouds,

And flown down through the Skies! It has driven its talons deep into the head

Of the Angel who is bound to the rocky mountainside, tore the Angel's side

With its sharp beak, is now biting at his festered dark red liver!

The Angel of Suffering writhes, making the rock shake with his convulsions,
    thundering noises making the air tremble,

Echoing through the mountain! The Sun is suddenly covered with clouds,

And cold winds are blowing by the dark mountainsides!

Ah, the holy Angel has stopped moving, and finally his head has drooped down.

Will the dead Angel ever come back to life like Christ?

ANGEL OF JUSTICE

Oh, you, of little faith, do you doubt the resurrection of the Angel

Who has accomplished his mission and dedicated himself
    with his sacrifice of Love?

The Angel who died to redeem the Sins of human beings is favored by God
    and is resurrected.

The Angel of Redemption is related to the Lord Christ's Suffering

And is resurrected at every dawn of the purifying night of the Passover.
Thanks to the Redemption and Revival of the Helping Angel
     who is with human beings,
The minds of human beings are allowed to keep working.
But human beings' hearts are apt to forget the Forgiveness granted
     by the Holy Being's Redemption,
And easily fall into sinful Temptation, made arrogant by thinking
     of their own abilities.
Relying on their own Power, discarding Reason which is their true mate,
Their hearts unite with the voluptuous Insolence that tempts Desires,
Keeping the alluring Devil that continues to breed Vices in their hearts.

Therefore, future human beings, driven by their Desires, will seek Pleasures,
Devouring the resources of the Earth, and keep polluting and hurting the Earth.
Human beings found Copper and Iron which were easy to stretch and spread,
And then Gold and Silver, and dug up the ores which had contained these minerals,
Since early times, and washed them in river water, smelted them in fires
And processed them. Consequently, the water and earth were contaminated.
And those who dug up the ores died from the minerals' poison.
The human beings of the Future will cut down more trees in the forests,
Dig up more mineral deposits relentlessly, and, scattering more poison all around,
They will become sick and suffer.
And also, the human beings who had found burnable stones and liquid
Used them for fuel since early times, and the human beings of the Future
Will dig up more black stones and draw up more black water
From deeper underground and with the fire they make by burning them,
They will continue to warm rooms, smelt metals, and operate what they contrived.
The fossils and sap of the plants which have been buried, disintegrated,
     and transformed since ancient times
Will be awakened from sleep, exposed onto the ground,
By the Greed of human beings,
And the obstinate Soot of the deadly Coal and the deplorable Exhaust

of the deadly Oil
Burned by human beings will hover and cover the Skies,
    and keep tormenting human beings.
The temperatures of the air holding the heat of the Sun will rise,
And all the creatures breathing in it will gasp in high temperatures.
The human beings who had burned the primeval forests planted crops
There, but the human beings of the Future will seek even more Profits,
And will not give the land rest, thus abusing it.
They will exterminate insects by using chemicals,
The Poison will invade into the soil, damaging it,
Dissolving into water, contaminating wells, ponds, and rivers, too.
The Poison that has remained in crops will revenge itself by hurting human bodies.
The undissolved Poisons discarded by human beings in huge quantities
Will dissolve in the final Grave in the distant Seas,
Accumulating in the fishes and sea shells,
And will return to the bodies of the human beings who eat them.
Forests will be cut down, blighted in black rains,
The soil will be washed away, and ruined deserts will expand.
Marshes and rivers of fresh water will be polluted and dry up.
Thus, birds, animals, and human beings too will gasp for the water of life.
The coral trees in coral reefs which are the homes of many living things
Will die out, turning into forests of white bones,
And the gorgeous World in the Sea will turn into a Grave at the bottom of the Sea.
By the actions of human beings who have kept hurting the Earth,
Many species of animals, microbes, and plants will perish,
And the Earth will lose its wholesome, beautiful Harmony,
And expose its ailing shape to the human beings of the Future everywhere.
Together with Nature ailing and weakening,
The bodies and minds of human beings, which are parts of Nature,
    will fall sick and weaken.

Even while the ailing conditions of the World advance,

Shady businessmen, disregarding the Earth's injuries, rob Nature
    of its resources,
And in order to build up enormous Wealth,
Use the labor obtained at low cost, produce newfangled goods,
And sell them by stirring up the Desires of human beings
And obtain enormous Profits.
The skills of building up Wealth and Profits will captivate human hearts,
And they will come to believe in Money ever more and worship it ever more.
Human beings will become the slaves of Wealth,
Running around, looking for wealthy people's leftovers.
The City of Prosperity will shine in the Sun by day, and with artificial lights
    by night.
And at the bottom of the prosperous, consuming City
Poor people's tattered huts will endlessly extend.

Ever since ancient times, haughty Emperors have let the people dream
Of the Future Prosperity of a strong country,
Made warriors of young men,
And, looking for fertile land of other countries,
Have taken the land with Spears and Swords under the pretext of Justice.
The Emperors of the Future will use the Devil's Vehicles
The Tubes, large and small, which can shoot off Evil Bullets in rapid succession,
The Huge Iron Elephants which trample down human beings, spitting Fire,
The Steel Sea Animals which will dash and smash enemy positions,
The Metallic Murderous Birds which drop Bombs,
Which their egotistic, clever brains will keep devising,
And will fight for Supremacy, looking for more land and resources on the Earth.
Mobilizing their arrogant brains, those in power will perfect a forbidden Bomb
Which will produce super-high-temperatures that can exterminate everything,
And detonate it in the Sky above the metropolis of an enemy country,
Burning up the streets and innocent civilians.
Human beings will keep killing each other in ceaseless conflicts, civil wars,

And occasional big wars, and refugees who have survived slaughters
      will drift over the ruined Earth.
Even if human beings are faced with a Critical Time of Life or Death,
Powerful persons in strong countries will build fortresses
Not only on land and sea, but also in dust-covered Skies,
Looking for planetary territories and resources,
And will scheme to monopolize even Outer Space.

Even at a time when fighting is over,
Inner conflicts lying deep in human hearts will not cease.
The Desires of human beings are Wildfires that will never go out.
What will dash around in the Future World will be Vehicles of Fire
Operated by Monstrous Animals.
The Weird Animals will get fat, devouring Money,
Blowing the flames of Greed, gulping down newly-made Money.
Vehicles of Fire that have been running through several centuries,
Built upon the front wheels of Production and the rear wheels of Consumption,
Will keep speeding up, never stopping,
And if left to run free, will burn up the entire Earth,
Never stopping till they burn up themselves.
In the Vehicles of Fire, built upon the human right wheels
And the mechanical left wheels, only the left wheels will get larger,
And if left to run free, the Lopsided Vehicles will shake off
The numerous human beings who are holding on to them,
And will drive out of the traffic lanes along the cliffs,
Falling down to the bottoms of the gorges and burn out.
Even if the Critical Time closes in on human beings,
The Arrogant Brains of the Future will devise Artificial Intelligence
Which will take the place of the human beings,
And thus human beings will become the slaves of Mechanical Instruments,
And the Fire Vehicles, ever more lopsided, will speed up,
Blindly dashing into the unknown Future.

When the vital functions of Nature's Life grow weak,
They will recreate a New Living Creature out of the fragments of animals and
     humans,
Attempting to preserve and improve their species,
And will try to purchase Deathless Life with Money.
They will remain disturbed by the alluring whispers and voices
Of the Devil in their own hearts which will entice them to become Creators of Life
In place of their dead God.
Their Brains defeated by Temptation will try to create New Human Beings,
Violating the Law and committing the Forbidden Act of manipulating
     the Species of Life.

Even if human beings have committed Crimes to such an extent,
They will continue to live without perishing.
It is all because of the Redemption by God's Love
And the assistance from the Helping Angel that reenacts the Lord's work daily,
And all because the hearts of human beings facing the Critical Time of perishing
Will repent and return to the Right Way.
And, as stated in the Lord's parable in which the Prodigal Son almost starves
     to death
In a foreign land repents and returns to his father,
The hearts that repent of their Sins will be welcomed by the Lord and allowed
     to live.
The human hearts may regain Reason, and the human brains which have fallen
Into artful thinking through Arrogance and lost the Right Way of human beings,
May restore humans' Intelligence, equipped with Modesty and Moderation,
Led by Sagacious Conscience,
Lit by the Light of Wisdom, looking over the Way forward.

People basking in the morning Sun may change their cold, fossil-like hearts
Into warm hearts of blood and flesh. They may get off the Vehicle of
     Destruction,

Step onto the ground of the Dawning World,
Feeling its texture underfoot again, and slowly start walking.

They will stop and stand, healing the wounds of the Earth
        with their tears and sweat,
Healing the diseases of the Earth with Compassion and Care.
They will transform deserts into green fields, praise the revived flowers,
Listen to the songs of the birds that have returned,
And harvest the crops, the gifts of the Earth.

Those healed people will appreciate the revival of themselves and the Earth,
Praise the Light that brings Peace and Life.
Sensing the fresh breaths of green mountains and fields,
Human beings on the Earth will rejoice together, and dance and sing
        in a circle of flowers.

Those revived people will cross over national boundaries,
Holding hands together, become friends with peoples in far-off foreign lands,
Helping the poor, supporting the weak,
Sharing things with other peoples of the World,
Looking for a Truly Rich World, and will step forward.

New human beings will watch over the fertile Earth carefully,
Faithfully handing it down to the living things of the Earth of the Future,
And complete the Love of Justice.

More people will strive to build a World of Love
And live, devoting their daily labor.
They will know that they don't lose by giving but grow richer by giving,
Because it is Love that they give.
But, not many people may know it and practice it.
Dark forces will attack even traveling people.

Therefore, human beings on the Earth will keep fighting
With the Dark forces till the end of the World.
Only those who keep the Law of Love which the Lord commands,
     clothed in the protection of Love,
Will win the battle.

God created the Universe with the Love in which He gives Himself
And He rules it with His sacred Work of Infinite Love.
Therefore, all things in the Universe give way to subsequent phenomena.
They follow the nature of the inner Love given by the Lord, transcend themselves
And enter the Great World of Love, and work within it.
Even the infinitesimal speck of matter drifts
In the Universe with innocent Love.
Love is an act of giving one's whole being to others,
And is the Universe's unchangeable principle on which all things are connected
     with each other.

TRAVELING MONK

I have found anew that the Lord Jesus Christ dedicated Himself
As a sacrifice for redeeming the Sins of human beings
In order to save all human beings
And that human beings are forgiven and allowed to live on
Because of the Lord's precious Intermediation.
I have also found that in order that the human beings of the Future may be saved
They will have to repent their Sins of Arrogance and Greed,
Regain Reason, control their Greed, return to living in Contentment
Through Moderation, and live in harmony with the surrounding World.
I have also found that the Universe's Principle, following God's Will, is
That all things should give themselves to others with Love.
Even so, how can human beings be saved from the troubles
That occasionally attack them so harshly, even beyond the Sins of human beings?

For what reason are innocent people tormented with frequent Earthquakes,
    Tsunamis, and Volcanic Eruptions?

ANGEL OF JUSTICE

Violent natural phenomena are calamities in the eyes of human beings,
But they are not calamities in the Eyes of the Creator,
They are just the rhythm of the living Earth, just its Energy emitted.
Human beings should deal with these violent phenomena,
Using their Intelligence as much as possible,
And recognize them as trials of Life.
They should not resent or grieve over the violent motions of the living Earth,
Because Life was brought forth by Nature's irregularities
Which are alive in the Lord's Love.
Every being is changing in the rhythm of the Universe,
    forming and disintegrating,
In the constant alternation of Life and Death. An old being decays and perishes,
And a new being takes form and is reborn.
This rhythm of Life and Death of all beings is nothing but progress
    to higher beings.
Things that are given Life by Love are also given Suffering,
Because the Suffering in living turns toward the Great Joy of higher beings.
An old being disintegrating and perishing has a premonition of its new birth,
And the Suffering in existing will melt into the Light of Rejoicing a New Life.

I know about the Life, Disease, Aging, and Death of human beings on the Earth.
You must not run away from the Suffering of Living.
Human beings learn Wisdom through Suffering.
Whether one takes Suffering as an abominable Punishment of Life
Or as a proof of Endurance toward Light is a matter
    entrusted to each person's Free Will.
If possible, you had better dedicate Suffering to the Lord as an Offering,

And thus strengthen your Faith in the Lord and Hope for Life.
When Suffering is unbearable, you had better rely on God.
The inner God of the suffering people will take over the Suffering
And take it off, thus giving them Peace of Mind.
Even the greatest Suffering is not unbearable.
Endure Suffering. Accept Suffering, and throw your body and mind
Into the fire of Suffering.
The trials given by the Lord of Mercy is a road that is bearable,
        a road leading to the Light.
Violent flames of the Lord's Love will purify and discipline the hearts
Of suffering people, and their hearts will be refined and have
        the great Joy of Rebirth.
Needless to say, followers of Christ should know
That this road of Suffering and Death of the Passover is the road to Immortal Life.

In order to save all the beings that appear and perish in the Universe,
God gave His beloved Son to the Universe,
And the Incarnated Christ experienced sufferings with his own body,
Showing the road of Salvation, not only to all human beings,
But also to all the beings in the Universe,
The Cross of Christ is the Central Mark in the Universe,
Because all the beings in the Universe pass over the Suffering on the Cross
        and Death
And come to the great Joy of Rebirth.
Look! Look at the summit of this rocky mountain!

(*A light from Heaven lights up the dark summit of the mountain,
and an Image of Christ crucified on the Cross appears, surrounded
by a circle of Light.*)

TRAVELING MONK

(*To himself*) Ah, what a piteous figure! His blood-smeared head drooping,
Wearing a Crown of Thorns, his both hands and feet nailed down,
    broken and ripped with the weight of his body,
His whole body is so dangerously hung.
His body, writhing in pains, is spouting bloody sweat.
Shouldering all the Sins of human beings on his body,
Carrying all the Sufferings of the World, He is suffering.
Though it is daytime, darkness extends as far as the end of the Horizon!
The Lord's body doesn't move. With his Death on the Cross, He conquers
    all the Evils,
He is offering Himself as precious Sacrifice to God, His Father.
By offering this Infinite Love, He saves all the beings from Evils.

(*Suddenly, the glittering point of a spear pierces Christ's side,*
Blood and water spouting and dripping to the ground.
The Monk, prostrating himself, keeps praying.
After praying deeply, he again looks up at the summit and the sides
of the mountain.)

The figure of Christ on the Cross shining at the summit has disappeared!
Only the clear blue Sky is visible. The Helping Angel bound to the rock
And the Angel of the Great Eagle by its side, too, have disappeared!
The rocky mountainside is basking in the Sun, shining brown, silent!
What I have seen till this moment, was it a daydream, or just an illusion?

(*The Monk walks back a little along the trail, and again looks into the cave.*)

Oh, I don't see the old man! The white cloth he was wearing
And the straw mat he had on the floor have been folded and put in the back.
He must have been relieved of the torment of the disease's severe pains,
Through God's help, and must have walked down this rocky mountain.

Now I know that this rocky mountain has become my Holy Land.

A Holy Land need not always be the famous land of pilgrimages.

A Holy Land is in every place,

Because when God visits a human being's heart, the heart becomes a Sacred Place,
    a Holy Land of the heart.

May the Holy Land of my heart not be stained, and may it continue to be
    a Sacred Place.

Oh, the range of surging mountains, great gorges, seas of green trees, green fields,

Villages here and there, all these are basking in the Bright Light,
    peacefully breathing.

May this peaceful scene, bathed in the bright Light in front of my eyes, continue
    to be the Peaceful Scene of my Soul!

Far on the yonder side of these great highlands extending as far as the Horizon,

Mt. Ararat is shining white. It is a magnificent natural Sanctuary,

Ennobling Heaven and Earth better than any great sanctuary in town.

It is a Sacred Signpost showing the long journey of the pilgrims.

The plain I am headed for is still far away.

Now, I would like to go down the mountain trail quickly,

So that I may get to the monastery at the foot of the mountain before sunset

And ask for lodging overnight.

II

A Dramatic Poem: *ZEAMI*

Characters: Traveler
             Old Man
             Ghost of Zeami

Place: Sado Island

Time: Early Autumn in a Year toward the End of the Twentieth Century

Act I   The Seacoast of Nanaura[1]

(*A traveler, carrying a rucksack and a sleeping bag on his back, appears on the road by the seacoast.*)

TRAVELER

When I stand by this rugged seacoast with its strange-shaped rocks,
     how good I feel!
My petty self is broken by the sharp fangs of the white waves attacking the rocks,
And the cold sea winds coming a great distance over the ocean waves are
     ceaselessly blowing through me,
Through my body and mind, and I seem to have entered into a spiritual state
Of perfect selflessness in which the foams of my idle thoughts vanish.

Look, there is someone in the rocky place. Is he playing among the reefs at low tide?
It seems he's coming up with something in his hands.

(*An old man who looks like a fisherman appears, holding a fish basket and a gaff in his hands.*)

OLD MAN

The sky looks calm today, doesn't it? Is there something I can do for you?

TRAVELER

Hello. No, not particularly.
I was enjoying myself, just watching the white waves
Coming in and the wide expanse of the rocks. What can you catch here?

OLD MAN

Here we get laver, nagamo seaweed, ginba seaweed in winter,
Wakame seaweed and sea lettuce in spring,
Mozuku seaweed and rock oysters in summer,
And turban shells and octopuses in all seasons.

TRAVELER

It's a good fishing place here, isn't it? But, isn't this rocky place dangerous?
You look quite old.

OLD MAN

No. I'm quite used to it. This isn't just my pastime here on the seacoast.
I get my food here. You are a traveler, aren't you? Where do you come from,
        carrying all those things?

TRAVELER

I sailed across from Niigata[2] to Ryotsu,[3] lodged in a hut, went over the mountains,
Came down to Nyuzaki in Sotokaifu, stayed at the campground, and then
Walked and took a bus along the seacoast, passing through the old town
Of Aikawa, and now I've come to Nanaura Seacoast here.

OLD MAN

Oh, it's a big journey. And, where will you go today?

TRAVELER

After taking some rest here, I plan to go around Daigahana Point,[4] and then to Sawata[5].

Today I plan to pitch a rental tent at the campground and spend the night.

OLD MAN

You're a tireless traveler, aren't you? I'm going to take the shellfish I've caught
To the inn at Tachibana Point. Would you go part of the way with me?
There's a bus that runs from Tachibana to Sawata, you know.

TRAVELETR

That sounds good. I'd like to go along with you.

(*The two men go up to the road above the seacoast and the old man moves
his shellfish from the basket to the fish pen on his cart by the road.*)

OLD MAN

The things on your back must be heavy. Why don't you put them in the back space
Of my cart?

TRAVELER

Thanks a lot. In return for your help, let me help pull the pole of your cart.

(*The two men grab the poles side by side, and start pulling the cart.*)

You're working so hard. You're strong in spite of your advanced age, aren't you?

OLD MAN

Even when you are old, you should use your mind and body. Your legs get weak

First in your old age, so I try to use my body as much as I can, walking
Instead of riding on a bus. Working, taking a rest from time to time,
Is the best way to stay well, you know? A good worker can enjoy the rest
Of his life, you know? You walk so well. Do you live in a city?

TRAVELER

I come from Tokyo. When I was young, I used to trek in the mountains,
So I'm used to walking. As I was working for a company producing beverages,
I used to walk in the mountains, testing the water quality of the springs and streams,
Both for practical purposes and my pastime.
But, due to this recession, the company I had worked for many years went
Out of business, and I lost my job. So, this has become a journey for thinking
        over my future life.

OLD MAN

That's a big trouble, isn't it? Just like a roof-stone falling from a roof.
By the way, are you a bachelor?

TRAVELER

No, no. My wife is working for a company, and I have a son,
        a third-year college student,
And a daughter, who is an eleventh grader. My wife is a contract employee.
Her pay is small and her position is insecure. As I am unemployed now,
My family members are all worried about our future life.
Due to this terrible recession, my son is afraid he may not be able to get a job,
And my daughter is worried, wondering whether she should go on to college
        or find a job.
Even so, since I became jobless after the age of 40, I've taken this opportunity
To look back on the first half of my life and find a way for my family

To live together. So I've come on a trip by myself and I'll keep walking
       around Sado Island.
When I was working for the company, I commuted back and forth
       between my home and office,
Riding on crowded trains, morning and evening,
I was used to the crowds and noises of a big city, but in my travel on Sado Island,
I walk through the deep forests of big trees, crossing mountain ridges,
Looking at blooming flowers in the fields, fresh spring water gushing out of rocks,
The deep blue ocean, and white waves breaking on the rough coast.
When I find myself in all these things, I feel as if my primitive senses
       have been revived, and my vital, fundamental powers for life awakened.

OLD MAN

Good for you! Mountains and seas, away from the city, have powers to heal
Human beings. A big city eats away at human beings' minds and lives.
It's a terrible place. It's a terrible place where the power of money pulls
And sucks everything in like a whirlpool.
In the last war, many young people were taken into the military service,
Sent over to foreign lands and they didn't return to the island. I was so lucky
I didn't get killed on the battleground. After returning to the island
After the end of the war, I was employed by a fishermen's boss
And worked as a fisherman. Then I got married and a son and a daughter were born.
When my boy finished his high school and became a fisherman,
I borrowed some money from the Fishermen's Cooperative, bought a small boat,
And we, my son and I, worked hard together at fishing,
But it didn't last long. The boat was damaged badly in a typhoon
And we couldn't go out fishing any more.
My son said that he wouldn't continue as a low-paid hired fisherman
And that he would go out to a big city to make and save money
So that he could buy a boat after paying off the debt.
So he went to Tokyo to make money.

He was working as an employee of a construction company's subcontractor,
But one year later he got killed in an accident at the construction site,
　　　while working on a bridge girder.
It was so sudden that I didn't get to see him at his death.
Just because I let him go to the city, I had him die in the prime of his youth.
When our daughter got married and went to Niigata, my wife and I lived
　　　by ourselves.
We two went out to the seashore to get seaweeds and seashells.
My wife was a hard worker. As we lived by the shore, she went out to Kun'naka
And worked, staying there in the autumn harvest time.
We raised some vegetables in the back garden.
We had no lack of food, thanks to her work, you know?
My wife was such a healthy person, but she fell sick five years ago.
It was so painful that she couldn't even turn over in bed.
She couldn't put food in her mouth, got thin, and died at last.
My longtime companion has gone, gone over to the other side of the sea.
As she never came back again, I felt really lonesome.
After that, I have lived by myself.
My daughter is worried about me and asks me
To come over to her place in Niigata, but this way of living is carefree.
As I am still in good shape, I'm working like this.
My home isn't the only place that has become lonely. Young people have left
　　　the island,
And only old folk work on the farms and catch fish.
Young folk don't take over the family's traditional work.
Every village has fewer people now. We have big roads all around the island,
And big ferry boats bring lots of cars,
But regular bus service on the island has decreased steadily,
And we old folk have difficulty getting around.
Roads have improved, and more travelers come to Nanaura
To view the sunset and it's good to see the inns at the points doing good business.
While the travelers have increased, the local people of Sado Island have decreased.

What will become of Sado Island, when those folks die?
Since early times we have gotten much rice and good vegetables on the island
And we can catch lots of fish. If you go out to the mountains and fields,
You can enjoy watching lots of flowers. You can live an easy life here,
So I wish the young folk would feel attracted to the island,
Where life is more valuable than money. But, if still more people leave the island,
I want to have lots of city people like you come over to the island.
Then everyone on the island will have a better life.

Now we've come close to Nagate Point. You'd better take the bus from Tachibana
To Sawata. There should be a last bus service of today.
When your bus goes around Daigahana Point, you will see an inlet.
From there you can see the pinewoods of Koshi in Sawata on the other side.
When I was a kid, my grandpa told me that a learned Buddhist monk,
A deportee lived, in a hut in the pinewoods in olden days.
As Mano[6] on the yonder side of Sawata is a place where many deportees
        used to live
In olden times, you should visit the place and dedicate your thoughts
        to those souls.
Thanks a lot for pulling the cart all the way to this place.
I'll go to the inn at the Point to deliver these things before I go home, all right?

TRAVELER

Thank you very much for your valuable talk. Meeting you on this trip
Has been a once-in-a-lifetime experience for me, which I'll never forget.
Please excuse me now. I'll take the bus to Sawata. Well, please stay well. So long!!

OLD MAN

I hope this trip will bring you good luck. Well, continue your journey
        in good health. Goodbye.

Act II   In a Tent in the Pine Woods of Sawata

(*The traveler is taking a rest after eating a simple evening meal in the rental tent he has pitched on the campground.*)

TRAVELER

(*Aside*) What a peaceful evening! The sound of the waves on the beach,
And the sound of the winds in the pinewoods I hear from time to time calms
   my mind.
The sun has set, and crickets have begun singing in the grass of the cool woods.
The dark night is closing in, but the light of a single candle on the dish is good
   enough for the little space of the grassland.
In this secluded place, I feel as if I were sitting in a relaxed position
In my own room with my natural mind properly restored,
Even though I am in a place far away from my home.
Well, I'll boil some hot water on the camp stove and make tea.
Before setting out this morning, I stopped by a farm house and got this
   fresh water out of the well and put it into the bottle.
After losing my job I started on this journey, looking for a way of life
And came over to this island where many deportees had been expelled
   in olden days.
It must be by some strange chance that I am spending a night in this place,
Thinking of the deportees of olden days.
If a deported Buddhist monk had lived in a hut somewhere in the pinewoods
In olden times, just as the old man I met on the Nanaura Coast,
Who walked part of the way with me said, tonight I would like to offer a cup of tea
To the soul of the pure-hearted, selfless monk, and it would be most appropriate.
I'll use this cup for a vase, and put a wild chrysanthemum I picked up in the woods
   in it.
I'll use this small dish for an incense burner, and offer some incense.
Now, the water is boiling. I'll make tea with this pure hot water and offer

A cup of tea to the soul of the monk.

(*After offering the tea, the traveler drinks some tea, and then he puts out the light, rolls himself up in the sleeping bag, and goes to sleep. Awaking from sleep at midnight, he finds it light in the tent and gets up.*)

TRAVELER

How come it's so light? It doesn't seem to be the light of dawn.
It's still deep at night, but the moonlight shining in through the small window
has made it so light.

(*The man opens the entrance of the tent and looks out.*)

The full moon hangs in the sky, the fresh light comes through the treetops
    of the pine trees,
The woods loom up white, and insects in the grass are singing
As if they were competing with each other.
Night dew in the grass is shining white. All the empty space nearby is lit up
By the moon, and it looks especially light.
It's a sin not to bask in the moonlight on such a beautiful night like this.

(*The man puts on a jacket and goes out of the tent.*)

Act III   An Empty Space in the Pinewoods

(*The man moves closer to the empty space and sits on an old bench in a corner of the moonlight.*)

TRAVELER

Look! The middle of the space seems especially bright. Is it filled with white fog?
No, a thin white robe is lit up white by the moonlight.
I can see something like a human figure through the white robe.
A human being seems to be standing in the moonlight in the empty space.
Hello, why are you standing there,
In the woods at such a cold midnight? Do you live near here?

GHOST OF ZEAMI

Who is calling me from the woods? Are you a traveler who is staying
        in the pinewoods?
Why should I hide anything, now that I've come down to the human world?
I'm the ghost of Zeami, who was lucky enough to be born into this world
In the olden days of the Muromachi period,[7] and learned as much as I could
        in the art of Noh.
A little while ago, a white chrysanthemum appeared from below , shining
Into the World of Light in Heaven, joining the infinite array of Heaven's flowers
Of varied colors, tenderly emitting a fresh fragrance.
And also a sweet scent of burnt incense came up from below,
Wonderfully mixing with Heaven's superb scent, soaking into the robes
Of Heavenly beings and Heavenly maidens, and pure hot tea spouted out
From a sacred fountain, and I came to the holy fountain
With the flying Heavenly beings, and drank the exquisite savor of the holy water
And danced. I was happy about your thoughtful heart for holding
        a memorial service

In honor of the gods and Buddha. While dancing, I looked down
      on the human world
And I saw a soft streak of incense, a flower, and smelled the aroma of tea,
Rising from the pinewoods on Gold Island where I had spent some time
While I was alive. I remembered I had spent some time on that island,
And that I sat and meditated in a thatched hut in the pinewoods,
Offering incense, flowers and tea to the gods and Buddha, and to the souls
Of dead people, and then I wondered how someone came to hold
      a memorial service
For me now, after the passage of many generations, and in order to meet him
And thank him, I have flown down from Heaven to the pinewoods lit up
By the full moon on this dear Gold Island.

TRAVELER

(*Aside*) Ah, what a strange happening! This famous person from the distant past
Has appeared so unexpectedly and is speaking to me!
(*To the ghost of Zeami*) Just as you say, I am a traveler staying in the pinewoods.
I knew by reading books that you had been deported to this island long ago.
But I never knew that the person to whom I offered the incense and a flower
Was none other than you. Please forgive my thoughtlessness.
I heard a legend that a deported monk had lived in a thatched hut
In the distant past, and I thought of the monk and just offered incense,
A flower, and tea in my tent tonight.
And being jobless and helpless, I am wandering, looking for a way of life.
I am especially thinking of how the deported Buddhist monk trained himself
      in the place of exile.
So, intending to look into the Master's way of training, I held a simple
      memorial service.

GHOST OF ZEAMI

Since a memorial service for a deceased person is an act of praying
For his peaceful repose in the other world, his heavenly bliss increases.
If the heart that is holding the memorial service is broad,
All souls in Heaven receive its blessing.
It is said that the Merciful Heart of Buddha, which is boundless,
Saves even lost souls in the Nether World.
Those who are seeking the Teachings of Buddha
Should hold a memorial service with a spirit of salvation for all the deceased.
Since the gods and Buddha accept the spirit, not the substance,
A spiritual service is favored. An old sutra says that a lantern offered by a poor man
Is superior to ten thousand lanterns offered by a millionaire.
Celestial beings rejoice when a lantern lit by a sincere heart
Ever increases the Light in Heaven.
Since a memorial service is conducted by a person's inner Buddhahood
And its eventual result is to enter into the State of Enlightenment,
Holding a memorial service is certainly a part of seeking the Truth.
If you are seeking my way of life, I will meet you at your memorial service,
And tell you about the way I have taken in my lifetime.

TRAVELER

You are such a precious, virtuous person.
I am so grateful to you for giving me your precious power.
This happy occasion must have been granted by Buddha's Providence.
I will hear your talk respectfully.

GHOST OF ZEAMI

Generally speaking, a monk's training isn't limited to conducting
   sacred services in the temple,

It also includes the basic movements of walking, stopping, sitting and lying
 down,
And moreover, living itself is the way of learning Buddha's way of living,
Whether one is a layman or a monk.
I was learning, trying to improve the Noh play in my lifetime, and I finally got
 to realize
That learning the art of Noh was none other than seeking Buddha's Way.
I naturally learned the art of Noh side by side with my father,
 since my early days.
I always learned by looking at my father, taking over the spirit and skills
Of the art, and trying to learn the art with all my soul.

Kan'ami,[8] my father, was born in Yamada of Yamato Province, became
 a Noh player,
Organized a Noh troupe at Yuzaki, working hard to raise the level
 of the Mimetic Noh.[9]
He took Icchu, a master of the popular Paddy Noh,[10]
As his mentor, and learned his artistic style,
Added the rhythm of Kusemai dance to the music of the songs of the Mimetic Noh,
Improved it to the level of delightful music, and it became popular and spread,
Which got to be known as "Tune of Kanze[11]" in the public.
The Troupe went up to Kyoto and performed their plays at temples and shrines
Here and there. Then they put on their plays at Daigoji Temple[12] for seven days,
And Kanze got to be known in the world as the "Master of the Mimetic Noh."
As a child, I went on the stage too, and was praised as a very good child player.
Ever since the Shogun's family came to see the Mimetic Noh at Imagumano
 in Kyoto,
Both my father and I were favored by them and the Kanze Troupe became
 ever more popular.

I was favored by high-class people of Kyoto, but I tried to be careful
 about myself,

Thinking that the beautiful cherry blossoms flaunting their beauty
In spring cannot remain beautiful forever, and that their beauty is only temporary,
And I cherished the art of Noh, chanting its chants in a fresh manner.
I diligently practiced to learn each and every form of dances perfectly.
A young main performer experiences the change of his voice and body
      at around 17 or 18,
And when his first blossoms fall, he feels ashamed of his awkward movement
      and dancing,
Losing his self-confidence, feeling disgusted with himself,
And surely he comes to feel like quitting the Noh stage.
Around that time, I made a vow in my heart that I would never quit the Noh stage
In all my life, and I followed the basics of training,
Intoning moderately, never forcing my voice, and I secretly kept
      training myself.
Just after dedicating the Noh play to Sengen Shrine in Suruga,
My father passed away at that place at age 52, and I took over the leadership
      of the Kanze Troupe, though I was young.

TRAVELER

When many Mimetic Noh troupes were competing among themselves,
You took over the Troupe at a young age, and you must have had many hardships.
How did you get over the trying times?

GHOST OF ZEAMI

The burden was heavy when I took over the Troupe after my father's death,
And I was overwhelmed by the difficulties expected in the future,
But, in the annual rituals at shrines and temples in Yamato Province,
I fulfilled my duty with the help of other troupes based in Yamato.
And we didn't compete with other troupes in Kyoto,
Instead, we went around the countryside

And gave performances to entertain country people, thus supporting ourselves.

The instructions left by my father were precious,

All the Troupe members supported me, patiently waiting for a new style
of mine to appear.

And, thus, at 24 or 25 my voice and body gained their stable forms, and I trained
myself with all my heart.

Generally speaking, if one wishes to become an accomplished master of the art,

One should make utmost efforts to expand the scope of his art

And raise the level of his art. This I have learned from the art of my father,

Who was the master of the right path of this art.

In order to expand the scope of my art of the Noh play, I learned the graceful style

Of singing and dancing from Inuoh of the Mimetic Noh of Ohmi Province,

Who was famous in the world in our times,

And later on, I learned a cool flavor of performing the Noh play

From Zoami[13] of the Paddy Noh,

Refining my style of the art open-mindedly.

And also, as my father considered it important,

I often visited the remote countryside

And performed the kind of play that the country people liked.

I learned on my frequent trips far from Kyoto

That the ideal state of the art should be like a clear mirror

That reflects the hearts of all people, irrespective of their social status high or low.

Moreover, I tried hard to learn many skills of mimicry, mastering every kind
of posture

And I practiced to become a perfect master of the art.

Also I tried not to forget the image of my previous figure in the past,

Keeping it at the present time and became a versatile leading player

And I expanded my art.

But the scope of the art doesn't end just with itself.

Since there are high and low ranks in every art,
Just as the priest who has mastered Buddha's Teachings is honored as a saint,
The superb master who has learned all the techniques of the art is honored
As a saint of the art. Just as a Buddhist saint who has attained
The state of Enlightenment and attained the rank of "Superbly Enlightened"
Leads human beings to the Light, the master of the art who has mastered
The special grace of the art leads the hearts of people to wisdom,
While helping them enjoy themselves.
The way of the art is none other than imitating the way of seeking
      the Teachings of Buddha.
Since there is such a precious value in the art of Supreme Intelligence,
Both the players and the writers should try to improve the art
In order to attain the Supreme Level of the art's Wonderful Flowering.
In the prime of my life I also learned Zen from the Chief Priest
      of Fuganji Temple of Yamato,
And then I sought the teachings of Zen masters at the Five Zen Temples[14]
      of Kyoto,
And savored Zen "Sayings" and "Quotations" over and over again,
Trying to master the way of the Noh play with all my heart.

However, as I looked at the way actors lived in those days, I noticed
They were not following the enlightened way toward making the art bloom
      into a glorious flower.
They neglected their training in the art. Following the ways of the world,
They looked for temporary applause just for one evening, fame just for one day,
And many of them showed their careless, premature acting in their Noh plays.
Even good players who had availed themselves of a good chance were misled
By their fame, feeling arrogant, forgetting their fresh, original intention,
Not perfecting a new skill, and not raising the level of their acting
To make their art bloom into a glorious flower.
Their acting of the Noh plays grew poor, and excellent players in the art
      became rare in the public.

Most of them were ignorant of the real essence of the art of Noh,
Neglecting their training, and wandering around in the dark.
The life of the art that is not nourished by its traceable source grows thinner,
And is destined to die and fall and decay. So I was afraid that this art too
Would come to its terminal stage, decline and perish, and I wrote down
The secrets of the art of Noh in various writings, so that I might hand them
Down to the successors for the sake of the art.

I didn't want to flaunt a temporary flower.
I wanted to seek the supreme level of the superb art
      with the heart of a lifelong trainee.
Since there were high-class people who loved my art, looked for knowledge
      about the Noh plays, and had a critical eye,
I tried to maintain the family tradition handed down
By my dead father, sticking to our principles in the face of the trends
Of the times, though in the uncertain world.
My eldest son, Motomasa,[15] was also well versed in the Noh art,
An excellent leading player, and he was also good at writing Noh plays.
He showed his masterful talent near the prime of his life,
And so I handed down my title, "the Headmaster of the Kanze Troupe" to him
Without any worries, and I became a monk, looking after the Troupe
And working hard in handing down the art of Noh to others.

Then came the winter in which cold winds raged furiously.
The new Chief of the Muromachi Shogunate was a man possessed
Of deep obsessions. My son and I were planning to go to Sento Palace
To present a favorite Noh play to the ex-emperor, but we were told
Not to carry out our plans by the Shogun, perhaps because he wanted
To exercise his political power even over the performing arts.
Moreover, I was dismissed from the post of the director of the Noh play
At the Seiryugu Hall[16] of Daigoji Temple, and was replaced by On'ami,[17]
Who was favored by the Shogun's family.

My second son, Motoyoshi,[18] was a drummer of the Troupe,

Showing his talent as a writer of Noh plays,

And he was terribly worried about the future of the Troupe,

Because its performing activities in Kyoto came to be prohibited by the
Shogun,

And so he became a monk, escaping the weary World after compiling my talks
on the Noh art.

In less than two years later, Motomasa, who had succeeded the title

Of "the Headmaster of the Troupe" went down to the countryside
to perform some plays,

And while he was traveling around in Ise Province, he passed away at Anotsu.

A letter conveying this sad, sudden news arrived.

One's life is destined by Providence, and our life and death cannot be foreseen.

But if one's child dies suddenly, one feels indescribably sad and helpless.

I thought of the chagrin of my son who didn't get to live his future,

And I wet my robe with tears in the dark of night.

Feeling so sad, my old body got weaker, and my heart sank into utter dark.

I felt my body and heart decaying.

The temple bell at night sounded as if it were mourning my own death.

Though he was my son, he had become an incomparable actor,

And all the secrets of the performing art I had written down and given him,

My successor, had become only transient dreams,

Only destined to disappear as useless dust.

With the early death of Motomasa, our way of performing came to an end,
our Troupe perished.

Only my miserable old life remained. I felt so sad, having such hardships now,

Oh, how miserable my old life became!

TRAVELER

(*Aside*) Ah, what a mysterious figure of this precious celestial being!

66

The human figure seen through the thin robe is violently shaking,
His face looking down is touching the sleeves of his robe!
Even the bright moon that lights up the autumn night has hidden
Behind the clouds! Chilly winds suddenly blow wildly in the pinewoods,
And the trees are swaying, while letting out sad screams.

GHOST OF ZEAMI

Since these memories are too impressive, they suddenly revive in my heart!
And my heart is caught in the web of attachments, turning into a beast
    of earthly desires,
Carried in the fiery cart of delusions, spurting flames, miserably tossing around.

TRAVELER

(*Aside*) The celestial being has transformed himself,
Putting himself in the raging winds, fluttering his robe which has turned scarlet,
His hair violently flying in all directions, holding bamboo grass leaves
    in his hands,
Wearing the mask of a grudging Devil, running around the empty space,
    dancing madly!

GHOST OF ZEAMI

Winds are raging violently where my confused mind is wandering in the dark,
My body is enveloped in burning flames,
Dayflowers trampled underfoot are burning in the wildfire,
The tree I am clinging to turns into a pillar of flames,
Receiving the fateful punishment of extreme heat,
I move around madly, finally falling into the eternal fires of Hell.

(*The celestial being stops his violent movement and turns his face down.*)

There now, Buddha's round Halo shines on every corner of the World,
Accepts all the human beings invoking Amida Buddha,[19] not rejecting
    any of them.
When the Light of Amida Buddha shines even on the paths of Devils,
I am brought back to my senses suddenly, and reflect on myself,
And suddenly the violent flames of Hell have turned into cool breezes.
I feel as if my body has been refreshed and brought back to life,
And I have realized that an old mind's obsession is the gravest obstacle
    at my life's end.
Thus, I have repented, sat and meditated, and my mind has regained peace.

TRAVELER

(*Aside*) Now, without wearing a mask, the merciful-looking celestial being
Is dancing with his white robe spread wide. What an exquisite, elegant figure!
The black storm is gone, the waves of the sea have calmed down,
The Full Moon is shining brightly in the clear sky,
Lighting up the pinewoods peacefully, where cool night breezes are blowing!
After finishing his dance, the celestial being stands in the clear Moonlight.

GHOST OF ZEAMI

Even if the flowers of the performing art have fallen, if the hearts
Of the later generations take over their seeds, the life of the art will revive
Sometime in the later world with the help of the gods and Buddha,
Blooming abundantly, emitting a sweet scent.
I should entrust the art which has gone away from me to the gods and Buddha.
What is the good of lamenting over the loss of the art of our family,
Vainly wasting days and nights? When I am old enough
To foresee the remaining years of my life, it's a regrettable sin
To waste precious time, without carrying out the most important activities

of spiritual training.

Now that my activities in the performing art have come to an end
And my heart has been released from its bonds, I have come to realize
That I should start training myself, fully using every moment,
Without relying on the performing art, and I have started to learn the Teachings
Of Buddha with my original eagerness.
Therefore, when I got the word from the Muromachi Shogun
That I was to be deported to Sado Island, God knows for what fault,
In less than two years after my son's death, I set out for the Island of exile,
    without lamenting the adversity,
Without losing my usual frame of mind, entrusting myself
To the course of Nature, because I had almost renounced the World.

We took a boat from Kohama of Wakasa, looking up
At the snow-capped Mt. Hakusan in the distance,
Sailing along the long seacoast of Noto, passing by Suzu Point,
Leaving the fishing lamps behind in the dark,
Then looking up at Mt. Tateyama at dawn, and soon we arrived
At the Ohta coast of Sado Island. Then, going up and down the mountain trail
    after dawn,
We finally arrived at the place of exile named Shimpo at night. I stayed
    temporarily at a small temple there.
However, fighting broke out on the island and my place of exile was involved
    in the fight,
And I ran away westward, to a temple at a place named Izumi,
    seeking a dwelling.
I finally got used to the lonely way of living, and at the discretion
Of the landlord there I was allowed to go out freely, and so,
I visited the old sites of temples and shrines in the vicinity,
    consoling my heart from day to day.

At one time, when I heard that the grassy field near my abode had been

The site of the palace of the ex-emperor Juntoku,[20] I visited that place.
In the dreary field on an autumn day, I saw that the pillars of black timber
Of the ancient palace had decayed and disappeared,
And only wild grasses were growing. Even the singing of the insects
In the grasses was feeble.
Standing in the dreary autumn winds, I thought of the sad conditions
Of the deported ex-emperor of the past. Did the ex-emperor sit alone
In the drafty, humble hut, never forgetting about the Capital,
Wetting the sleeves of his robe?
If the emperor's heart was as clear as the bright moon reflected
On the fresh water of a fountain, the road of burning flames in daily hell
Must have turned into a cool road for Enlightenment and his disturbed mind
Must have been calmed down, thus allowing him to escape the weary world
        afflicted with hardships.
On another occasion, I made a long journey and visited and worshiped
        the famous Buddha there
In the old mountain temple named Hasedera.
As the shape of the temple and the scene around it looked just like that
Of the Hasedera Temple of Yamato, I felt as if I had returned to my home,
And so I visited this sacred place from time to time.

As there were many shrines and temples on this lonely remote island,
With the gods and Buddha nearby, I worshiped them, offering my dances,
And I prayed for the peace and safety of my family members, far on the other side
Of the white clouds and countless waves.
Ujinobu,[21] our daughter's husband, the Headmaster of the Komparu Troupe,
Often offered his kind help to my wife, Juchin, at a far-off place,
And also to me on my journey, and I was so grateful to him.
Consequently, I was able to live, feeling relieved with a peaceful mind
        in the place of exile.
Some local people saw my chanting at a temple or a shrine,
And I occasionally taught chanting and dancing to some people who asked me

to teach them.
Many of them brought some money or garden products, and moreover,
They rebuilt the dilapidated, empty hut in the pinewoods by the bay,
And presented it to me.
As the years vaguely passed by, I sat and meditated at the Buddhist temple
In Izumi or at the thatched hut in the pinewoods, visited temples and shrines
    all over the area,
And kept dedicating my dances to the gods and Buddha in this charming place.

(*After keeping silent for some time, the celestial being lightly stamps his feet
beating time, and stretches forward his right hand, which is holding a pine twig,
and turns it around.*)

TRAVELER

(*Aside*) Ah, the celestial being is slowly beginning to dance!
Even in the sphere of reminiscence, the immortal power of Song and Dance
Is making the celestial being dance, isn't it?

GHOST OF ZEAMI

(*The ghost of Zeami begins to dance and chant the first part of the dance solemnly.*)

When the sky above the mountain lightens at dawn in spring, golden clouds hang,
And a white mist rises over the wide plain, and snow water glistens in the streams.
With the chanting of the sound of the pure streams and the flute
Of the morning wind coming over the mountain,
I dedicated my dance to the spring Sunlight shining on the young grass
On the ground, in praise of the Way of Heaven.

On a beautiful spring day I went to the seaside, stood by the rocky seashore
Upon which white waves were sweeping, and looking over the rapid current

full of fishes,
I danced to the roaring sounds of the Sea, considering them the chantings
        of the Dragon God,
Dancing to the drum of the furious waves beating on the rocks,
Looking toward the Light shining brightly from the end of the Sea,
Dedicating my dance to the gods and Buddha who mercifully give us groupers,
Praying for safe fishing in the Sea, praying for calming down the winds.

When clouds of cherry blossoms covered distant mountains,
I was tempted by the cherry blossoms, and quickly set out with a merry heart,
And going along the mountain trails, I saw the spirits of all things
In the bright cherry blossoms falling and fluttering in the wind
And enjoyed looking at the wild flowers blooming and falling in the fields.
But I realized that the image of the Flower of Light appearing
        in each and every heart
Is none other than the Eternal, Immortal Flower.
And I turned into the spirit of cherry blossoms in the Sky, and I danced
To the flute music of the stormy winds going over the mountains,
Blowing down the cherry blossoms, the dances of "Peace in Transience,"
"Joy in Transformation," and "Flowers scattering in Buddha's World,"
        not knowing whither I was going,

Assuming that it might be my last chance to savor the departing spring,
I went out to the fields where flowers were abundantly blooming
In the gentle winds to talk with the flowers of various colors,
And when I got into the woods of green young leaves lit in the Sun,
I danced at the fresh-aired shrine to the flutes and drums of the mountain birds
Which were freely singing, and to the chanting of the loud sound of the stream.
I stood by planted rice paddies in gentle breezes, praying for a rich crop
        of golden rice.
I danced to the loud chanting of the frogs in the distant paddies

as far as Heaven
In praise of all the green mountains as far as I could see.

On a bright summer day, I looked for a cool spot and I chose shade,
Visited a shrine in rich green, and saw a newly-wed couple visiting the shrine.
I stood in the shade of an old, strange-shaped cedar, holding *sakaki* leaves
In my hand, and I dedicated my dance in honor of the God,
Chanting that we should praise the mysterious work of the God residing
In the sunlit shrine on the island and uniting all things in the World.

On a hot day, I walked over the fields where summer grasses seemed peaceful,
And went up the hill looking over the Sea and Mountains.
And stood in the Holy Light of Mt. Hakusan's Sacred Image
Far at the end of the Sea from which pleasant winds were coming,
And I looked up at the shining clouds
Which made a halo for Mt. Kimpoku,[22]
And from afar I reverently admired the magnificent mountain grandly depicted
	in Heaven
And I dedicated my dance to the God.

When the wind was chilly in early autumn and I felt pensive,
I went through the woods where evening cicadas were singing
And visited the deserted tomb of the ancient emperor.
By the light of the weak, flickering flame of a watch fire in the evening,
I dedicated a dance as a memorial service to the flute of the voice
Of a woodpecker hidden in the backwoods of the dark shrine
And to the drum of the evening bell of the mountain temple.

In an evening when the Sky was clear in high Heaven,
I went out as far as the shore of Misaki Point
To view the Mid-autumn Full Moon, and danced to the faint Light

Of the Sun setting on the other side of the Sea,
Worshiping the Pure Land in the West.
When night came, the Full Moon hanging high in Heave shone
Brightly over the peaceful Sea,
And to the rhythmic beat of all the waves coming in and drawing back,
I dedicated dances of "All-Pervading Light" and "Religious Ecstasy."

When autumn deepened, I saw off the birds sailing in the Sky,
And fondly praised the light of the dayflowers in the fields.
I went into the mountains, where tree leaves were changing their colors.
When the bright, flaming red leaves fell silently and shone on the ground
        covered with fallen leaves,
I saw the moving shadows of the gods and Buddha in the constant transfiguration
        of all things.
In the singing of the birds and in the sound of the mountain streams,
I heard sermons of the mountain and water and I danced the dance:
"The Praise for the Marvelous Law of Buddha."

When winter came, and on a day after a stormy wind, I went into woods
        of withered trees
And caught winter's deep light in the red nuts of a thorn.
In the stillness of the dead valley, where the dimly-lit image
Of a mountain bird moved and rotten tree leaves piled up,
The glow of every perished thing increased, and I was enveloped
        in a blinding Light,
And I dedicated dances of "Nirvana's Light" and "Aspiration for Rebirth."

At the beginning of the New Year, I got up at dawn, drew fresh water,
And in the fresh morning, I visited the shrine brightly covered
        with white snow and I danced,
Praying for "Peace of the World" and "Happiness for All Human Beings."
Like a flower blooming on the rock enduring winds and frost,

I still had a flower of my heart in my old body, and so it was my real wish
To celebrate everything with all my life and praise the gods and Buddha.

On an extremely cold night in the quiet World in severe winter
I got away from things, from human beings, even from myself,
And stood in the frozen field in the light of snow, looking up
        at the clear Milky Way.
I walked forth onto the grand Stage of Silent Heaven to the accompaniment
Of the chanting voices of the countless stars dimly blinking and the Music
Of Heaven's exquisite melody, and danced the dances of "The Realization
        of the Exquisite State" and "Bliss of Light."

(*After dancing in a state of Heavenly Ecstasy, the celestial being, remains
silent for a while, and then begins to speak.*)

Thus, I kept dancing the dance "Joy of Outing" and was spending the remaining
        part of my life with a peaceful mind,
Realizing that it was by the divine will of the gods and Buddha that I was brought
        to this place
To attain the highest level of my art and complete my life.
However, something strange happened at the Muromachi Shogunate
        unexpectedly,
And I was notified that I had been released from my deportation.
I had formerly decided to make this island my burial place and I was used
To the way of life on the island, but I thought that the pardon too was Providence
And that I only had to obey it. So, I made up my mind to go back to Yamato,
My home, where my son-in-law, the Headmaster of the Komparu Troupe,
My wife and daughter were living.
Since I was pressed for money, I danced religious dances at the shrines' festivals
For about a year, taught the landlord the Noh dance at his request,
Saved travel expenses, and also some help came from my son-in-law,
And I finally got my journey ready and took my leave of the local people

Who were sorry about my parting, and thus in order to leave this Gold Island
Where I had come to feel at home by then,
I set out on a journey for Yamato, together with an attendant.
The long journey was hard on me, an old man over eighty, but I made up my mind,
Thinking that it would be Heaven's will even if I fell on the road,
And I only thought of easing the minds of my wife, Juchin, my daughter,
And my son-in-law, who had been waiting for me anxiously,
And continued my journey with all my might, and thus I finally arrived
      at my home, Yamato.
Not long after meeting my family happily at our humble home,
My old body grew weak and I fell sick in bed.
Soon I realized that the end of my life wouldn't be far away,
So I went out for my final meditative concentration,
And when I innocently looked at the Moon of Absolute Truth which had risen
I was lit by the Light of Mercy
And my mind was completely liberated.
As a memento of my farewell to you, I would like to reenact the scene,
Showing you how my clear mind was lifted toward the Light of the Great Mercy
      in the Vast Sky.

TRAVELER

(*Aside*) Ah, with his robe of feathers widely spread,
The noble, celestial being's transparent body is emitting light and pulsating!
Stretching out his hands gently, he has calmly begun to turn over the grassland!

GHOST OF ZEAMI

My detached mind of religious concentration sees:
Mountains of Yamato and Kii provinces nearby.
The valley of the Seto Inland sea route in the distance,
Provinces spreading over toward the Western Sea,

Distant sea routes at the end the North Country,
The Gold Island floating on the Sea far away,
And in the Northeastern provinces, I can see a long range of mountains,
Holy mountains here and there, wearing white robes, above the clouds.

The scenery changes, lit up in the Merciful Light of Perfect Freedom,
All the mountains, fields, and vegetation which calm down my heart
        are emitting Light from within,
Nurturing my mind and body, making the World majestic with Boundless
Light,
Brightly lighting up my way, while I go, adoring the Beautiful
        and aspiring for the Sublime.

Reflected on the mirror of my mind are foods from the Sea and Land,
Flowers, fruits, grains, birds, beasts and livestock, all of these have
Fed the ancestors of human beings and my father and mother
        who begot me and raised me,
And I have seen that all the things in the World past and present
And all the living things emitting Boundless Light have nurtured my life.

The Merciful Light of all things in the Universe has ever increased,
Expanding to the boundless Sky, advancing quickly, enveloping my mind,
Transforming my desire for detachment into a Light,
And my mind rejoices together with the Milky Way of Lights of all things,
And has been pulled to the very Source of Boundless Light.
The Light of my mind longing for Light returns to the Source of Light
        in this way.

    TRAVELER

(*Aside*) Ah, The celestial being's body shines ever more brightly,
And he soars upward from the Ground,

Gently fluttering his robe of feathers,
Dancing upward round and round like a white Heron!
What a Holy Dance!
This is certainly the Dance of the Exquisite Flower in Heaven.
All the stars in Heaven are shining and sparkling,
Welcoming the soaring Flower of Heaven.
Oh, the celestial being who soared upward has disappeared into the starlit
Sky!

(*The man sitting on the bench wakes up.*)

Well, I must have fallen asleep while I was unaware.
Was I dreaming a long dream while sleeping on the grass at midnight?
Did I make up a story unconsciously and see it in my brain in a dream?
Or did the celestial being really come down and tell his stories in a dream?
Either way, it seems the True Way that I had been seeking on my journey
Was suggested in the dream. Tonight will be a night I will never forget.
The Moonlight has already become weaker, hanging above the mountains,
And the remaining Stars are about to disappear.
The eastern Sky is dyed in the color of dawn.
It seems the day has dawned.
Today, I will visit Shoubouji Temple in Izumi, where Zeami had lived,
And think of the Master of the art, hold a memorial service
For the teacher of Life, and pray for the repose of his soul.

Notes prepared by the translator

Zeami (1363-1443?) One of the most important Noh players, a prolific Noh writer, a critic. Became a Zen monk in 1422. Wrote 21 critical writings and many Noh plays. Was exiled to Sado Island in 1434

(1) Nanaura: In the western part of Sado Island.

(2) Niigata: The largest city in Niigata Prefecture on the west coast of Honshu, the main island of Japan, facing Sado Island to the west

(3) Ryotsu: A main seaport in the northeastern part of Sado Island

(4) Daigahana Point: The southern tip of the western part of Sado Island

(5) Sawata: In the central part of Sado Island on Mano Bay

(6) Mano: Also in the central part of Sado Island on Mano Bay

(7) the Muromachi period: Ashikaga Takauji, (b.1305-d.1358), the first Shogun of the Muromachi government, established the government on Muromachi Street in Kyoto in 1338 and a total of 15 Shoguns maintained the Muromachi government till 1573.

(8) Kan'ami (1333-1384) Zeami's father. A Noh player and writer. His ordinary name was Kiyotsugu..

(9) the Mimetic Noh: Widely used humorous mimicry in movement and speech

(10) the Paddy Noh: Performed in the rice planting time.

(11) Kanze: Zeami's father, Kan'ami was also known by the name of "Kanze."

(12) Daigoji Temple: Built in Kyoto in 874

(13) Zoami (b.?-d.?) A Paddy Noh player, known for his cool, elegant style of performance

(14) the Five Zen Temples of Kyoto: Tenryuji, Sokokuji, Ken'ninji, Tofukuji, Man'juji

(15) Motomasa: Zeami's eldest son (1394?-1432)

(16) the Seiryugu Hall: Built for a worship hall at Daigoji Temple in 1597

(17) On'ami: A Noh player, Zeami's nephew (1398-1467)

(18) Motoyoshi: Zeami's second son (?-?)

(19) invoking Amida Buddha: People repeated intoning "Amida Buddha, Amida Buddha...," asking for help and salvation. Amida Buddha is said to rule the Pure Land in the West.

(20) ex-emperor Juntoku: (b.1197-d.1242) 84th emperor of Japan (1210-1221). Defeated in the Conflicts of 1221, exiled to Sado Island and died there.

(21) Ujinobu: (1405-1470), Zeami's son-in-law

(22) Mt. Kimpoku: In the western part of Sado Island

AFTERWORD: How These Poems Came to Be Written, and Their Subject

The subject and form of these two dramatic poems in this book may seem strange. Therefore, I would like to explain the process of my writing these poems and the theme which I have intended to write on, and also make some comments on these poems.

I have watched Noh plays performed on the stage ever since I was in my thirties, and I have read Noh books, and have become fond of the world of the art of Noh. Its strong charm lies in its incomparable artistic beauty, produced by the perfect unity of poetry, music, and dance performed on the stage, and its profound power of expression in its simple form. I had vaguely expected to create some dramatic poems which would have some Noh-style beauty, though I hadn't exactly intended to put them on the stage, and I jotted down some ideas whenever they occurred to my mind, expecting to use them as materials for poems in the future.

The materials which I had written down for dramatic poems had remained unused in my notebooks for many years. But something unexpected happened, and one of the materials put forth buds. Just after I had published a collection of poems on the history of the universe, three years ago, I fell seriously sick and I had an operation. On my sickbed, I laid the pains of my sickness on top of Christ's suffering on the Cross, and meditated on the secret meaning of suffering. In my convalescent stage, I connected the notes on suffering which I had put down in my sickroom with the materials based on the Promethean myth, and I thought of writing a poem.

The material was intended to imitate a two-act dream-like Noh play, using the following story. A traveling monk, who corresponds to the supporting player in a Noh play, meets a local old man, who corresponds to the leading character of Act I in a Noh play, in a mountain of Caucasia and is taken into his hut. The old man treats the monk kindly and tells him that he lives by himself in the mountain hut, enduring his sickness, and that his sickness attacks him periodically, and he asks the monk to pray for recovery from his sickness. When the monk goes up the mountain trail the following morning, the ghost of Prometheus, who corresponds to the leading character of Act II in a Noh play, appears bound in flames on the rocky mountainside. To the surprised monk's inquiry, Prometheus tells him that he has been undergoing sufferings in order to redeem the sins of his beloved human beings, ever since the primitive ages till the present. While the monk is praying, the flames on the rocky mountainside disappear, and shining clouds envelop the ghost of Prometheus and carry him off to Heaven.

When I started to write the dramatic poem, I realized I had been preoccupied with the form of a two-act, dream-like Noh play. The myth of a demigod, Prometheus, who undergoes suffering as a punishment for giving fire and skills to humankind, has become the subject of philosophy and literature ever since ancient times in a story that symbolizes the destiny of human spirits, and it has brought about diverse interpretations with changes in human spirits in history. I felt that the historical significance of the development of human spirits contained in the Promethean myth and the profoundness of its thought were in need of being expounded. Liberated from my adherence to the form of the two-act, dream-like Noh play, I greatly changed the materials of the dramatic poem while writing.

Because the subject of suffering which I had started with had developed from the level of an individual to include the sufferings of nations, and even of all humankind, the local old man in the previous act stopped being a mere sick person, and became a speaker about war and peace, through the perspective of the histories of the peoples in Caucasia and Palestine. Later on by expressing the sufferings of an old man by means of the sufferings of the old man who groaned in the cave of the rocky mountain, I tried to make its dramatic effect even stronger.

Furthermore, I developed the image of Prometheus and changed it into an angel who helps the human spirit develop, and I let the angel who is suffering in trying to redeem the sins of humankind speak of the history of human hearts. Moreover, I brought in an Angel of Justice who speaks of the destiny of human spirits and the necessity of spiritual conversion and tells about the secret meaning of sufferings and the way of salvation.

As a result, it has become a poem which has a free structure in which each character develops the story from his own viewpoint. Through the experience in writing, I have learned that the form of the dramatic poem has a dramatic element which expresses the present state of human wills and actions and that, in addition, it can become a flexible and broad-minded form which can make the co-existence of the epic-like element which describes the development of events objectively and the lyrical element which expresses the emotions of personal experiences subjectively possible, and thus can expand the thoughts and feelings to be expressed and bring in plural voices.

Believing in the possibility of the dramatic poem, I continued to plan to create another poem in the same form. The subject matter of Zeami follows the model of the two-act, dream-like Noh play. In this form, the leading character of Act I is an ordinary person, a human being of this world, and he expresses the real conditions of his life. The leading characters of Act II are a demon, an angel, a ghost, a spirit and such, and they fly through time and space freely, and by their language and symbolic movements, like spiritual beings, they reproduce the past of their lives, or bring their conditions of the spiritual world into the present. This kind of strong contrast in the framework of the play strengthens the dramatic effect of the two-act, dream-like Noh play. In the process of creating a dramatic poem which is not intended for stage production, a dramatic contrast in form has been lost, but it has become a poem in which each character speaks from his own position and viewpoint.

From the viewpoint of literature, the dream-fantasy Noh play has the form of a fantastic story. A dream has a way of expression which can be widely used in major literary styles, such as drama, lyric, and epic. The literary arts of the modern and present-day era have widened the territory of the dream and developed diverse dreams; such as bad dreams expressing the grotesque and horrors, fantasies getting away from everyday life and exploring a surreal world, and daydreams producing a dream-like atmosphere. Generally speaking, the dreams that appear in the literature of the modern and present-day era wander around in the conscious field of the senses, which may show that the literary minds of the modern and present-day era have attached too much importance to the sensory areas. The function of warning us of dreams which are born out of unconsciousness and can be called the remaining voices of an oracle in a dream was highly estimated by ancient people and it is occasionally used in literary expressions today, but such dreams are no longer an important technique for expression in contemporary literature.

But, the dreams which can be sublimated in literature and give public order in life have ethical and religious elements in them, and so I would like to place more emphasis on the function of such dreams which might work toward the future of spiritual life. Religious poems of medieval Europe envisioned a high dream in surreal time and space that could lead authors, audiences, and readers to a Paradise on Earth, and further to the light in Heaven, and they expressed them in the words of poetry. The dreamer in a literary work catches a glimpse of an ultimate scene at the end of the dream, awakens, and receives a great comfort and a hope, and thus keeps on living in this world. The imagination which looks for a dream in this condition shows the movement of *metanoia*,(a change in mental attitude or religious conversion), and aspires to rise to the ultimate fantasy. On the other hand, the imagination which looks for a humble dream such as can be seen in much of the literature in the modern and present-day era shows the movement of *metamorphosis*, (a change in form or a magical transformation),and keeps on changing the form of fantasy infinitely, without changing its true nature.

I looked for poetry with a metanoia-type imagination and tried to construct a work, believing in the possibility of a high dream in literature. By using this ideal dream-technique, the plot and structural form common to the two poems in this book have been established. Both poems have a structure in which a traveler looking for a way of life experiences a fantasy on his journey and learns wisdom and truth about life, as told by spiritual beings, and keeps going on the journey. In the former poem, in the fantasy, the angels show the right way which a human spirit should take and in the latter poem, in the dream, a celestial being shows a way to enlightenment. Because the former poem has Christian thoughts in its background, while the latter has Buddhist thoughts, and especially Zen thinking in its background, they seem to express different religious, spiritual worlds, but they both have a common basic theme in that they strive toward saving suffering human beings. The former poem tells us that human beings can be saved by a change of heart and belief in God, whether on an individual level or on the level of nations or humankind, while the latter tells us that human beings can be saved by a change of heart and by training oneself in search of enlightenment. The story about Zeami after his exile to Sado Island can only be found in a preserved collection of short Noh chants and dances entitled *A Book of Golden Island* and a letter addressed to Konparu, the Headmaster of the Troupe. The place and the year of Zeami's death are not known and his real image in the later years of his life remains hidden in a veil of mystery. I envisioned and depicted a human being who trusted the gods and Buddha, who kept seeking enlightenment, and who was eventually saved.

In the former poem, the angels expound on the secret meaning of sufferings and tells about rebirth through sufferings and the Passover of death. In the latter poem, the celestial being talks about emancipation through meditative concentration which transcends sufferings. Even though there are religious differences in creed, language, and system, the transcendental effects of the religious spirit and the transcendental intention of religious life are common to all religions. The actual practice of living through religious experiences never stops seeking God or an Absolute Being in a transcendental way. The way of the monk seeking Christ, and the way of the Buddhist monk seeking enlightenment, may not be so different from each other. The spirit of literature living in the age of dialogue and mutual understanding between different religions tries to illuminate the common road of each religious life in such a way. I think the two dramatic poems have been an attempt to illuminate such a way.

Moreover, these poems suggest that there is a deep relationship between human beings and the natural world. The reader will notice that the blessing of the natural world which is the manifestation of the blessing given by Supernatural Being shown in the healing and salvation of human beings is commonly called out in both Act I and the latter Acts of the two poems, as a subsidiary theme. In each Act, it is suggested that a rich natural environment supports the body, the mind, and the life of a human being and that the life of a human being can be fulfilled with the blessings of nature. In the latter Acts of the former poem, I looked more deeply into the subject and described the reality of both the sick natural world and the world of human beings and demonstrated a vision of healing and salvation in both. In the latter poem, I offered a new theme of what the artist and art should be like, but this should be regarded as a subsidiary theme following the main theme, as long as I am considering the matter from the viewpoint of the art as a search after truth.

When I make a general survey as outlined above, it is obvious that the two poems have been constructed fundamentally as related works which share a common form and theme, and that's why I put them together in this book as related works.

When writing these works, I needed many documentary materials. For the former poem, I obtained a great deal of knowledge and information from the Old and New Testaments to begin with, as well as from research documents in the fields of theology, philosophy, history, and anthropology, and from geographical records, research books, and theses concerning Caucasia. For the latter poem, I consulted sacred writings of Buddhism, sayings of Zen, sermons of Buddhist priests, Noh plays, essays and talks on the Noh by Zeami, and research books on Zeami. And as for archaic Japanese, I consulted the waka, tales, and essays of the early medieval and medieval ages, and I used various dictionaries of archaic words, especially "*Jidaibetsu Kokugo Daijiten—Muromachi Period*—1-5. (*Dictionary of the Japanese Language in the Muromachi Period*)" (Sansei-do, 1985-2001). As for the dialect in the poem, I was able to use "*Sado Hogen Jiten, (Dictionary of Sado Dialect)*" by Sadayoshi Hirota (privately printed, 1974), which is a precious dictionary of the dialect of Sado Island and a research document.

A new artistic expression is a new spiritual life created by the artist's mind which has worked on the tradition of the spiritual heritage accumulated by the artist over a long period of time. It is a tradition in which art, religion, and philosophical thoughts live, built-in, in the mind. Creating and expressing in an art can be compared to conceiving and childbearing. The artist effaces himself, reducing himself to the level of nothing, thus deepening his relationship with his inner spiritual tradition, and creates a new objective spirit. This new living thing becomes independent, participates in the spiritual community, and tries to contribute to the progress of the human spirit from the standpoint of art, even if it is just in a small way.

Therefore, an artwork parts from the artist and sets out toward the future of the spiritual world. I would be most happy if these two humble poems could reach the hearts of unknown readers and give them sympathy and a real hope for life.

Finally, I would like to extend my heart-felt thanks to Mr. Hisao Suzuki of Coal Sack Publishing Company for giving me advice and writing a commentary on this book. And I would also like to thank all the staff who worked for bringing this book to completion.

June 2017
Saburo Moriguchi

ABOUT THE AUTHOR, SABURO MORIGUCHI

Saburo Moriguchi was born in Tokyo in 1935 and educated at Kyushu University where he majored in English literature and took a B.A. and an M.A. From 1962 to 2001, he taught at Kochi Women's University, Saga University, and Ehime University. He published a collection of tanka, *Sankeishu* (*Mountain Paths*) (1992); a collection of essays, *Seiou Geijutsu eno Tabi* (*Journey to Western Arts*) (1995); a book of criticism, *Yamai to Bungaku* (*Sickness and Literature*) (2000); a book of poems, *Tamashii no Uchu* (*The Universe of the Soul*) (2014) and a book of dramatic poems, *Junan no Tenshi • Zeami* (*The Angel of Suffering • Zeami*) (2017). He passed away on June 3, 2019.

ABOUT THE TRANSLATOR, NAOSHI KORIYAMA

Naoshi Koriyama was born in 1926 on an island named Kikaijima in the Amami Islands between Okinawa and the main islands of Japan. He studied at Kagoshima Normal School 1941-47, Okinawa Foreign Language School 1949, the University of New Mexico 1950-51, the State University New York at Albany 1951-54, where he started to write poetry in English. His publications include: *Like Underground Water: The Poetry of Mid-Twentieth Century Japan*, co-translated with Edward Lueders, (Copper Canyon Press, 1995) and *Japanese Tales from Times Past* co-translated from *Konjaku monogatari shu* with Bruce Allen, (Tuttle, 2015) and *A Fresh Loaf of Poetry from Japan*, a collection of his poems old and new, (BookWay, 2018). Some of his poems have been reprinted in school textbooks in America, Canada, Australia and South Africa. He also participated as a translator in such anthologies as *Against Nuclear Weapons* (2007), *Farewell to Nuclear, Welcome to Renewable Energy* (2012), *A Collection of Poems for Independence, Freedom and Requiem of Vietnam* (2013), *Pains of East Asia* by Hisao Suzuki, (2019)—all by Coal Sack Publishing Company. He taught at Obirin Junior College 1956-61 and at Toyo University 1961-97. He is a professor emeritus at Toyo University.

ABOUT THE EDITOR, BRUCE ALLEN

Bruce Allen is a professor in the Department of English Language and Literature at Seisen University, Tokyo, Japan, where he teaches courses in translation and environmental literature. He has specialized in the writing of Ishimure Michiko and has translated her novel *Lake of Heaven* (Lexington Books, 2008) and a documentary film about Ishimure, *Toward the Paradise of Flowers* (Fujiwara Shoten Publishing Co., 2014). He has co-translated with Naoshi Koriyama a collection of ninety tales from the *Konjaku monogatari shu*, a medieval Japanese collection, *Japanese Tales from Times Past*, (Tuttle, 2015). He has lived in Japan for over thirty years and has been active in studies of the literary humanities and in the Japan Association for the Study of Literature and Environment.

石炭袋

Saburo Moriguchi　守口三郎 英日詩集

Two Dramatic Poems: THE ANGEL OF SUFFERING　ZEAMI
劇詩　受難の天使　世阿弥

2020 年 2 月 10 日　初版発行

著　者　守口三郎　（著作権継承者　守口康子）
訳　者　郡山直
発行者　鈴木比佐雄
発行所　株式会社 コールサック社

〒 173-0004　東京都板橋区板橋 2-63-4-209
電話 03-5944-3258　FAX 03-5944-3238
suzuki@coal-sack.com　http://www.coal-sack.com
郵便振替 00180-4-741802
印刷管理　（株）コールサック社　制作部

装丁　奥川はるみ

落丁本・乱丁本はお取り替えいたします。
ISBN978-4-86435-427-1　C1092　￥1800E

Coal Sack Publishing Company
2-63-4-209 Itabashi Itabashi-ku Tokyo 173-0004 Japan
Tel: (03) 5944-3258 / Fax: (03) 5944-3238
suzuki@coal-sack.com　http://www.coal-sack.com
President: Hisao Suzuki

劇詩　受難の天使　世阿弥　目次

劇詩

受難の天使　世阿弥

守口三郎

劇詩　受難の天使

登場人物　旅の修道士
　　　　　土地の老人
　　　　　助力の天使
　　　　　正義の天使

場所　　　南コーカサスの山中

時代　　　十二世紀末のある年の初冬

第一場　峠へ通じる山路

（袋を背負い杖を持つ旅姿の若い修道士が山路に現れる）

旅の修道士

冬の日暮れは何と早いことか。私が北国の森を出立したのは
半年以上も前の五月。みずみずしい新緑の中　林の鳥たちが巡礼の
旅立ちを讃えて歌っていた時節。その後　大地を打ち焼く烈日と
吹きすさぶ疾風の夏の大草原を越え　秋の実りで黄金の波うねる
平野を過ぎて　早くも寒風叫ぶ白霜の枯れ野を横切り　ようやく
隊商とともに険しいコーカサスの高地を越え　さらに独りで
原野を進み　峠を越える山路を喘ぎ登るのも　はるかな聖地
エルサレムの聖堂に参詣し　新しい修道生活に入ってゆくため。
だが四季の移ろいのように　うつせみの生の日暮れは早い。
古人も多く旅に死んでいる。　思い立った勇躍の心は逸っても
大願の成就は　まだはるか彼方の目標。与えられた一日一日の命を
全うすることが　真の旅の道なのだ。
おお　迫りくる夕闇に　雪も降り出し　行く手を阻む。もはや
視界が利かない中を盲進するのは　勇敢ではなく　無謀の愚行と
いうもの。旅に死ぬ覚悟はあれども　思慮なく路上に凍え死ぬのは

天命ではない。早く岩陰を見つけ　冬山の夜の厳しい寒さを
凌がねばならぬ。

(前方に草籠を背負う老人が現れる)

　　　　　土地の老人

ああ　そこの旅の方　こんな日暮れに　どこへ行きなさる。

　　　　　旅の修道士

この山路が思いの外に険しく　峠を越える前に日が暮れてしまい
雪も降り出したので　身を潜める洞穴か岩陰を探していたのです。

　　　　　土地の老人

それは無謀なこと。雪の降る山の夜の酷い寒さに　あなたの体は
耐えられまい。それに　この山中は　夜の闇に狼の群れがうろつく
危険な地帯。今日の仕事を終えて　近くの小屋に帰るところなので
私に付いて来なさい。谷間の狭い粗末な荒屋だが　寒さを凌ぐに
充分な筈。

　　　　　　　　　　旅の修道士

ご親切ありがとうございます。(傍白) この老人の助けも　私を
守護する天使の働き。まことに全知全能の神は　地上の小さい
存在をも慈しみ　細やかな心遣いを為し給う。神の摂理の
言い尽くせぬ尊さよ。私が捧げうるのは貧しい祈りだけ。
神の御心が万事に行われますように。

第二場　谷間の小屋

（老人は谷間の木立の中の小屋に修道士を案内する）

　　　　　　土地の老人

この丸太小屋は二部屋だけの簡素な住まいとは言え
烈しい風を避け　谷川の流れるこの土地を見つけ　強い日差しと
仮宿として四十年前から建て始めた小屋。　もともと狩猟の
建て増し　この老体と同じく古くなったが　まだ住める造りです。
日が落ちて暗くなったので　先ずは明かりをつけましょう。

（老人は箱から取り出した火打石と鉄片を打ち合わせ、火花を
火口に移して油皿に火を灯す。　次いで囲炉裏の粗朶（そだ）に点火する）

さあ　旅の方　この火に当たり　冷えた体を暖めて　ゆるりと
寛ぎなされ。　夕食の支度をしますので。

（炉の上の自在鉤に掛けた鍋に羊の干し肉と野菜を入れて煮る）

この谷は　沢の水が大地を潤し　霧が立ちこめ　日もほど良く

射しこむので　山菜　茸が多く　畠の野菜も良く取れ　色づき
彩り豊かな秋の森は　梨　くるみ　栗　すもも　葡萄など
木の実で満ちるのです。ここでは野菜を植え育て　茸や木の実を
採って貯えておけば　万物の精気が痩せ衰え　地に籠る冬でも
食物が底を尽くことはありません。

畠の野菜も　牧場の羊も　森の木の実や獣も　大地の尊い恵み
神様からの贈り物。山の民は　これらの命を与えられて生きている。
羊の脂は　この灯の油となって　光で闇夜を照らしてくれる。
それゆえ山中の独り暮らしに不自由はないのです。

（老人は煮えた鍋物を鉢に盛り、壺のワインを杯に注ぐ）

さあ　簡単な鍋物ですが召し上がれ。　先ずワインで乾杯しましょう。
この土地は　大昔の洪水が地上を覆ったとき　水の退くアララト山
の頂きに漂い着いた箱舟を降りたノアの一族が　虹のかかった
肥沃な大地で葡萄を作り　ワインで酩酊したと言い伝える葡萄の
名産地。地元の者は皆　自らワイン造りを楽しんでいます。

　　　　　　旅の修道士

自足の生活を楽しんでおられるとは　何と恵まれた境地でしょう。
その昔　極熱の砂漠　険阻な岩山　荒海の孤島に籠もった
聖なる隠者たちのように　ご老人も　この人里離れた山中に

隠者の生き方を求められたのでしょうか。

土地の老人

いや　私は世捨て人ではない。若いときは村で猟師として暮らし
良い連れ合いにも恵まれましたが　早く妻に先立たれ　独り者に
なったのを機に　狩猟に便利な山中に住居を移したまでです。
今は谷間の日当たりの良い空き地を少し耕し　野菜と山で採った
薬草を植え育て　時おり山を下りて　薬草を村里の薬屋に売り
市場で羊の肉などを買って帰るのです。村での商いの後は
商人たちと茶を飲むのが楽しみで　伝え聞く遠い異国の様子から
世界の有り様が良く分かる。

旅の修道士

私は　この山国から出たことはないが　その若い身で　ただ一人
旅の苦難も厭わず　どこから来て　どこへ行かれるのか。また
この土地のアルメニア語を話されるが　この山地の若者ではなく
異国からの旅のお方のようだが。

私は　聖地エルサレムを目指し　遠い北の国から旅して来た者です。
キエフ公国が骨肉の争いで十以上もの小国に分裂し　抗争で国は
乱れ　人里離れた森の修道院も荒らされたので　それも閉鎖され
ある者は故郷に帰り　ある者は北方に移住し　それぞれ四方に

散りました。
身寄りのない私は　北国との交易でヴォルガ河畔の町に滞在して
いたアルメニア商人の下で二年ほど働き　アルメニア語を習得して
コーカサスからアナトリア地方に至る道と町の様子　さらに隊商の
事情なども教えられ　聖地への巡礼の旅に備えたのです。
ようやく今年の春　ヴォルガを下り　夏の牧場で働き　秋の畠の
収穫を手伝い　シェマハの町で西方へ旅する隊商の雑役に雇われ
大コーカサスの連なる白銀の高嶺を右手に仰ぎ見ながら　商人たち
とともに交易の道を進み　ティフリスの町で西の　トレビゾンドに
赴く隊商と別れ　その後は一人旅で　各地の修道院に泊めてもらい
ながら　南コーカサスの山地を越えて来ました。
これから先は　アニ　ビトゥリス　エデッサを経て　アレッポから
南に下り　聖地エルサレムに至る旅路を辿ろうとしているのです。
聖地では　聖堂の修復　また巡礼者を救護する奉仕を果たした後
古代から修道士が隠れ住んだという険しいカルメル山の修道院に
入るか　その道が阻まれるならば　海路ギリシアに行き　聖なる
アトス山の修道院に行き　北国の修道院では
ギリシア語をしっかり学んだので　その経験が役立つでしょう。

土地の老人

（傍白）正しい目標を持って雄々しく生きる青年の姿は何と美しい
ことか。青年は清澄な光を輝かせながら昇る太陽。青年の秀麗は

かれらだけが戴きうる生命の花冠。しばしば思慮は怖気と手を結び惰眠（だみん）の寝床に潜りこむ。勇気ある青年の思慮は情熱と結びついて生き生きと活動し どんな困難をも切り開いてゆく。この力こそ青年の栄光というもの。

（修道士に）賢明と勇気の徳が働いて 初めて命がけの長旅ができるのでしょう。巡礼の道も昔に比べて より危険に満ちているようですが 用心して行かれるが良い。

十字架の徽章を身につけた狂信の軍兵の大群が 百年前に西方から遠征し 攻略したアンティオキア さらにエルサレムの都で大虐殺と略奪を重ね シリアとパレスチナの住民を追放し 土地を奪ってから もともと異教徒に寛容だったイスラム教徒の心に侵したキリスト教徒への憎しみが生まれ 積年の恨みが深く根づいたのも当然です。

近ごろ和睦が成立して休戦となり 聖地巡礼への自由も保証されていると聞いていますが その和平も永くは続かないでしょう。

一時の平和は 時勢の好運な巡り合わせを王たちが賢明に利用した結果。

我欲に目眩む権力者は 上辺の平和の綴れ織りを いともたやすく引き裂くし 平穏な王国も やがて強大な帝国の襲来で滅ぼされ その大帝国も命運が尽きると 内部の分裂 属領の反乱 異民族の侵入などで遂に命運が尽きてしまい 栄華の夢の跡の廃墟を曝すのみで剣を取る者は皆 剣で滅びると言われる通りです。

まことに平和の世は うねり動く時の中の微妙な均衡。絶えず変動する混沌の中から現れる一時の調和。動いて止まない平和をできるだけ保つには 若々しい精神の英知と機敏が必要なのです。

旅の修道士

コーカサスは 高嶺連なる険しい山岳地帯なので 異民族の野心を寄せつけず 山の人々は 不安なく末永く平穏に暮らせることでしょう。

土地の老人

いかに険しい山地も帝王の天を衝く野望を挫くことはできません。文明の十字路ゆえに コーカサスを幾つもの王国が支配しては滅びたと この土地の吟遊詩人も伝えています。また昔からさまざまな民族が豊かな土地を求めて 生活できる平地や谷間に住みつき 初めは多少の衝突や紛争があったとは言え 年月を経るにつれて生活の知恵を学び 平和に暮らす術を身につけたのです。今では異なる民族の村人たちが 親しく付き合い同じ宴に座して楽しみ 互いに婚礼や葬式にも参列しています。キリスト教徒もイスラム教徒も他の異教徒も 互いの信仰を認め互いの聖所を尊重しているのです。しかし時至って コーカサスの南北の大国が 互いに領土を拡げようと争えば この平穏な山地は 最前線の戦場となり

村人に災いが降りかかるのです。この地を征服した帝国の支配者が
横暴であれば　意のままに地域を分割し　抵抗する山の民を
虐殺したり　異教徒を追放して自国の民を移住させるでしょう。
その禍根から　虐げられた民のくすぶる遺恨が　憎悪の炎と
燃え上がり　後世に民族の間の紛争が絶えず　清浄の山地を
流血で染め　どす黒い悪念は　宿敵を呪い　過去を呪い続ける
のです。このような惨事も人間の性の為す業。
戦乱の心の傷は　長く人々を苦しめ続け　心が癒えるには
平和な三世代の歳月さえ充分とは言えないでしょう。

さて　話は尽きないが　茶を飲んだら隣の部屋でゆっくり
お休みなさい。明日の朝は早いので。幸いに降り始めた雪も止んで
明日は晴れるでしょう。とは言え峠を越えて麓へ降りる山路は
長い行程。余裕を持ってできるだけ朝早く出発なさるが良い。
この小屋から脇道を登って　元の山路に戻り　峠を目指すのが
最も確実です。明日の朝は　道案内も見送りもせず　失礼します。
訳あって明日は　ある場所に行き　十日に一度の定めの務めを
果たすために　夜明けの空が白む前から出かけねばならないのです。
もし山中で私を見かけても　決して近づかないように。
あなたの祈りに　私の心の平安のための祈りを加えて頂ければ
それで充分。それだけをお願いします。
明日の朝食と二日分の携帯食を用意しておきます。水筒には
この瓶の水を入れてください。礼金などは決して置かないように。

これからの旅に備えて　乏しい旅費を大切に。客人をもてなすのが
この土地の住人の心の誇りなのです。朝発つときは　獣が小屋に
侵入しないように　一戸のかんぬきを外から掛けてください。
明日からの長旅のご無事を切に祈ります。それでは安らかに
お休みなさい。

　　　　　　　旅の修道士

今夕は食事と寝所を与えて頂き　さらに明日からの食糧まで
用意して頂き　まことにありがとうございます。お話は
心の糧となりましょう。
あなたの心尽くしも　恵み豊かな神様の導き。一期一会の
この恵みを　私は生涯忘れないでしょう。事情があって
明日の朝は早出されるとのこと。これからも神様の慈しみが
あなたに豊かに注がれますように。末永いご健康と幸福を
祈ります。それではここで失礼します。お休みなさい。

第三場　山頂近くの小路

旅の修道士

（独白）ああ　有り難い。朝日が照らし　雪は溶け
白霧消える山路を　踏み行く足は　軽く弾み　澄める大気に
心も晴れて　爽やかに　光静まる山行く至福よ。
親切な老人の歓待で疲れも取れ　朝から好天に恵まれ
今日の山の旅は　はかどって午前中に峠を越えられよう。

この高い岩山を遠巻き迂回する路から　山頂へ向かう小路が
分岐している。どうしよう。このまま山路を進めば安全だろう。
だが小路を登れば　より広い展望が開け　地形も見て取れよう。
あまりに険しい路ならば引き返せばよい。天気も良く時間も
まだ早いので　この小路を登って行こう。

ここは頂上に近い岩場。遠くに越えてきたコーカサスの山脈
高原　牧地　白く光る川　眼下には　黒い森　深い渓谷が見える。
この世界の大空間に　明るい光が満ち　すべての物が
静寂に包まれて安らいでいる。

おや　かすかに物音が聞こえる。落石の音か。谷風の伝える
森の獣の叫び声か。いや　もっと近くから聞こえる音だ。
前方から聞こえてくる。岩角を切る風の音か。岩場に上がる
山羊の鳴き声か。岩穴に潜む鷲の声か。行く手の道端に
洞窟が見える。確かにあの岩穴から聞こえてくる物音だ。

（修道士は洞窟に近づき覗く）
光の射しこまぬ薄暗い洞窟の奥に　何か動いている。
鳥か獣か。おお　人が伏して呻いている。

第四場　岩場の洞窟

（修道士は洞窟の奥に横たわった人の傍に近寄りかがむ）

旅の修道士

もしもし　どうしたのですか？　ああ　何ということ。
この人は　昨晩私を助けてくれた老人だ。もしもし
私が分かりますか？

土地の老人

おお　業火に焼かれている私に　近づいてくる黒い影
おまえは誰だ。責め苦の炎で　身はぼろぼろに燃え崩れ
涙の干涸びた眼は　眩み翳んで　鼻先も見えないのだ。
おお　亡霊が私の手を握る！　槍剣の先の山地獄から来た刑吏か？
それとも　冥界から来た迎えの使者か？
どこへ連れて行くのか？　この火責めの生き地獄から
救い出してくれるなら　どこでも良い。さあ　早く出してくれ。
願わくは　もう苦痛のない冥界に連れて行き　静かな暗闇に
沈めてほしい。永劫の寂滅の空無に溶け込みたいのだ。

はて　耳元で呼ぶ声に聞き覚えが……現世に連れ戻すのか？
村の者なら　この墓穴に侵入し　冥土に旅立とうとする者の足を
引っ張るのは止めてくれ。火だるまで転がる私をどうするのだ。
おお　これは旅の若い人。どうしてここへ？　山中で私に
近づかぬように言ったのに。介抱は要らぬ。水筒の水も
くれなくてよい。山旅に必要な水は仕舞っておきなさい。
ただ私を独りにしておくれ。この惨めな姿を人に見せず
隠しておきたいのだ。

この病は　かなり前から十日ごとに襲ってくる業病
村の医者にも分からぬ病　自ら薬草を育て服用したが
薬も効かぬ不治の宿病。老いて近ごろ痛みがますます激しく
心が錯乱して　意識も薄れ　いつ最期が来るやも知れぬ。
もし　ここで息絶えても　戻って村人に知らせることはない。
この岩穴は　私の密かな墓場。果てて土と化すのは覚悟の上だ。
さあ　死骸同然の私に構わず　早く山を越えて行きなさい。

旅の修道士

（傍白）激痛に苦しみ悶える人を　私は助けることができない。
苦しむ人に寄り添うことも　時には邪魔になるのだ。無力な私に
何ができるだろう。今は　老人のために祈るしかない。
この人の苦痛を取り除き　安らぎを与えられるように
神のご慈悲を祈り求めよう。

(15)

（修道士は洞窟を出て行く）

土地の老人

おお　痛い　痛い　痛い
全身を締めつける毒蛇が歯牙で咬み裂き
たかり這い回る虫らも毒針を突き入れ
筋肉を腐らせ食って行く。
絶え間ない敵の総攻撃を受けて
私の身体の城砦は破壊され　心の司令塔は打ち砕かれ
身も心もばらばらに崩れ落ち　天地を
赤く染めて　なお炎上しているのだ。
焼け崩れた肉体　溶けた脳髄よ　ここに執着せず
おのれを焼き尽くし　どこかへ消え失せろ。
地獄からの刑吏は　この生き地獄に帰ったか。
冥界の使者は　どこにいるのだ？
この苦痛の現実を　離れて冷然と見ているのか？
死の使者よ　早く来てくれ。
おまえの大鉞で　この燃えさしの生命線を
すっぱり断ち切ってくれ。
……目先が暗くなってきた。
やっと冥府へ旅立てるのか。

ここはどこだ？　この薄暗い空間は？
もう冥界に入っているのか？
まだ意識があり　思考も働くので
死んではいないらしい。現世に送り返されたのか？
あまりの痛さで心が惑い乱れ　命を呪い
死を請い願って　あらぬことを口走ったのか？
激痛の嵐が一時去ると　狂気の荒天を
飛び回っていた意識は　明澄の
晴天の中　正気に帰る。
ここは洞窟の中だ。静まる岩穴に
前と同じく横たわっているのだ。

これまで責め苛む炎の中から叫んできたが
神は　沈黙したまま答えられない。
これまで苦痛のどん底から訴えてきたが
主は　暗黒の沈黙で覆い　答えられない。
ここは無限の地獄ではなく
煩悩を焼き尽くすべき煉獄なのか？

おお　有り難い。岩天井から滲み出る冷たい水滴！
この滴りを燃える舌で受けると　渇きは癒され
この滴りで　火照る身を濡らすと　焼ける痛みは鎮まる。

これこそ　神の恵みの聖なる霊水。

これが主のお答えなのか。この冷たい清水の滴りが。

主は　まだ私の身を焼き滅ぼさず

水で冷やせと命じられるのか。

おお　この沁み透る清水に洗われて　冷静な正気を取り戻し

黄泉の闇の入り口から　現世の光の世界に引き返したようだ。

灼熱の炎に跳ねて失神し　悪魔が取りつき

数々の汚れた罪深い言葉を吐き散らしたのであれば

主よ　哀れな私をどうかお赦しください。

主が私を決して見捨てず　主の憐れみで導いておられ

救ってくださることを私は信じます。

第五場　岩山の路傍

（洞窟の先を曲がった岩場の路傍で旅の修道士が祈っている）

　　　旅の修道士

（独白）この光は何だろう。瞑った瞼の裏まで明るむこの光は？

見上げる空は　いつもと変わらぬ青空だ。風景もいつもと変わらぬ

風景だ。だが　この辺りだけ異様に輝いているのは何故だろう。

おお　洞窟の上の山頂に近い岩壁が光を放っている。おお

岩壁に巨大な人影のようなものが張りついて光っている。

いや　自ら張りついているのではなく　目眩む光の束で手足が

岩角に縛りつけられているのだ。

あの光る像は何だろう。ギリシア神話の伝えるコーカサスの岩山に

縛られたプロメテウスの亡霊が現れたのだろうか。それとも

神に肩を並べようと思い上がった大天使が　天界から墜落し

この岩山に吊るされているのだろうか。

　　　助力の天使

この地に降りた私に問う者は誰か。この山地の民は　私が火を

もたらしたゆえに神罰を受け　岩山に縛られた太陽の子　反抗の
英雄アミランと讃え歌い　ギリシアの民は　私を主神に抗して
人類を導いた半神プロメテウスと讃え　私の責め苦を語り伝えた。
だが　私は天罰を受けたアミランでもプロメテウスでもなく
神に反抗して失墜した天使でもない。私は人類の心の発達を
助けるために付き添ってきた天使なのだ。

旅の修道士

おお　何たる不思議　いとも聖なる天使であるなら　純粋霊の
天使が　どうして人身の姿で現れているのですか？　また
人類の心の発達を助ける尊い天使が　なにゆえ　山の岩壁に
張りつけられているのですか？

助力の天使

そなたの疑問は尤もだが　純霊の天使が見えないとは限らないのだ。
天使の本質は霊であるゆえに天使の力は人の姿を
通しても働く。この世で働いている愛徳の人々を観るがよい。
また人々の模範となった聖者を観るがよい。また人が真心で天使の
助力を願ったとき　天使は瞬時にその人の心中に現れて力を与える。
天使は時として必要に応じ　人身の姿になることもある。
私が人の姿で現れ　しかもこの岩山の壁に張りつけられた異形の

姿で現れるのには　　特別な事情がある。その事の起こりを
そなたに語ろう。

主が人類の創造を決意し　霊長類の中から人類の祖先を選び
かれらに人間精神の因子を吹き入れられたときから　私は
人類の心の発達を導く使命を帯びて　天上界から地上に
遣わされたのだ。私は樹上のかれらに寄り添い　かれらの
心の成長を注意深く見守った。

陸地の気候が乾燥し　密林が減り　草原が広がるにつれ
最古の人類は樹を降り　草原に進出し　身を守るため後脚で
直立し　広い周囲を見渡し　二足で歩き走るに至った。
人類は命を守ってくれる群れを大切にして　その中で学び
能力を育てたのだ。かれらは自由になった前脚を手に変え
棒で根茎を掘り出し　石片で堅い果皮を打ち割り　捕らえた
小動物や死獣の肉を剥いで食べた。

見よ　人類は長い下肢　肥えた臀　広い骨盤　撓やかな脊髄の
上に大きい頭蓋と脳を載せ　神経網を豊かに張りめぐらせて
大地に立ち　私の力添えで思考と巧みな手先を働かせ　人類の
世界を拡げた。
かれらは木や石や骨角を加工し　さまざまな道具を作り改良して
植物を採集し　動物を狩り　食物を求めて移動した。かれらは
思い遣りと無意識の知恵で　乏しい食物を群れの皆に分けた。
知性を強めた原人たちは　伴う強い好奇心に駆られ　落雷で

燃えた森の残り火　火口から噴出し固まった溶岩流にも大胆に
近づき　神秘の火を薪に移して　住居の岩窟に運んだ。
かれらは火を絶やさず　暗闇を光で照らし　凍える身体を暖めた。
焚き火の炎は　牙を鳴らす野獣を近づけず　逆にたいまつを手に
獲物を穴や崖に追い落とした。捌いた獣肉を焙り　固い植物を
柔らかく煮て味わった。岩窟の聖なる火は　安らぎを与え
親しみ睦む家族の絆を強めた。

遂に　原人は知恵を働かせ　棒の尖端や石片を擦って火花を作り
乾い草や獣脂に点火し　天与の火を使い馴らした。光熱の宝の火を
手中に収めたかれらは　勇敢に獲物を求め　未知の大地　険しい
高地　北方の平原にさえ足を踏み入れた。氷期には獣皮をまとい
火を焚き　洞窟や仮小屋の中で　命の灯火を燃やし続けた。
夜の灯火に守られ　男と女は愛の炎の中で合体し　生まれた結晶の
子を抱き慈しんだ。乳児は微笑む母に微笑を返し　この愛の交流が
魂の根幹となり　幼児の心を養った。
父は　石器の作り方　装飾品の編み方を娘に教えた。
植物の採り方　狩りの仕方を息子に教え　母は　食用の
生活の技術と知識を正しく伝えるために　人は言葉を生み出し
子供たちにくり返し話した。かれらは　行動と言葉を通じて
技術と知識を学び成長した。
言葉は物の在り方を定め　物と物の関わり方も示した。
深い沈黙から発した真実の言葉は　千鈞の重みがあり　聴く者の

魂の深みに存在の光を伝え　彼の知性を刺戟し培った。
その結果　人類の感情は　より豊かになり　知性は進展した。
かれらは　親しみ愛した人の死を悲しみ悼み　来世の命を願い
遺体を花で飾り　副葬品を添えて埋葬した。
さらに　狩る人の群れに近づき殺されて肉を与え　人々の命を
養う気高い生き物　力と美と威厳に満ちた動物たちを　かれらは
畏れ敬い　洞窟の奥の岩壁に　命の供犠の聖なる動物たちを
命の血の朱色で彩り描き　その神性を讃えて祭った。
人々は風の音や雷鳴に主の声を聴き分け　太陽や月に昼夜の
神の眼差しを見た。かれらは　野に踊る花と戯れ　小川で
水を浴び　日光に裸身を曝しまどろんだ。
飢えれば動植物を求め　かれらを養う豊かな森の大地へ
移動した。無心なかれらは　主と天地の与える恵みで
万物と調和し　安らかに生きていた。私は人類の調和の
世界を祝福し　かれらの原初の楽園を見守っていたのだ。

旅の修道士

人類が創造されて以来　長い原始時代を経て　文化を創り出し
厳しい環境に適応して　神によって遣わされた尊い天使の導きで
知性を高め　感情を豊かにして　心を発達させたということは
分かります。それなら聖書の語る楽園の状態に置かれていた
人類が　なにゆえ争い憎み殺し合うようになったのですか？

なにゆえ至福の楽園から追放されたのですか？

助力の天使

その根本の理由は　人知の及ばぬ神秘なのだ。神の思いは
被造の存在である天使の知性をも高く超えるのだ。人が知り
えるのは　悪の在り様に過ぎない。人が引き付けられる悪から
離れるために　悪の実態を正しく知ることこそ人の本分なのだ。

人類は与えられた心を育て　その力を自由に応用し　生活の
範囲を拡げてきた。女たちは野草を栽培し　小麦に改良した。
人々は農耕や牧畜の技術を身につけた。こうして生活は
より安定し　子孫を増やした。だが生存の本能を超え
自己保存の意識を強めた人類は　欲望が募り　遂にうねり
渦巻く欲望の泥海から　魔性の我欲の毒蛇が躍り出たのだ。
定住した人々は想像を巡らし　不安な未来に備えた。安全のため
土地を所有し　食料や家畜を貯えた。所有は恐怖を増し　恐怖は
所有を増した。物を必要以上に所有し貯えると　他の部族の
略奪を恐れ　防塁を作り武装した。恐怖は不信を生み　不信は
敵意を生み　敵意は攻撃を誘発した。恐怖は悪心の母胎なのだ。
不安に駆られ盲目的な希望に縋って生きる人間たちは　競って
大河の潤す肥えた土地に住みつき　職業を分化させ　能率良く
資産を成して　砦回らす都市を建設した。やがて有力者が王と

なり　王は軍隊を組織し　他の都市を攻撃して　財を奪い
労働力の奴隷を獲得した。こうして人類は互いに攻撃的な
性格を強め　常に戦争が脅かすようになったのだ。文明社会の
悪が増しただけではない。個人の罪悪もまた増したのだ。
人々は　知力を尽くして世の富を求め　都市に集まり　快楽と
繁栄を願い　黄金の偶像を拝んだが　それも現世利益の物神に
過ぎず　人の心の悪への傾きは止まなかった。真の神に背き
独立を求めた人間たちの傲慢が　心の奥底に隠れ　もろもろの
罪悪を孕んでいたからだ。

月満ちて生まれた高慢は　虚栄心　名誉欲　自惚れ　利己心
冷酷な心を生んだ。嫉妬は　悪意　偽言　憎悪　呪いを生んだ。
不正な憤怒は　不和　侮辱　暴力　怨恨を生んだ。
貪欲は　利己心と交わり　財欲　支配欲　貪食を生んだ。
色欲は　淫乱　邪淫に堕ちた。心の怠惰は　節制を失わせ
人間を享楽の泥沼に耽溺させた。これらの罪は　機会を
窺って　密かに交合し　次々に罪を生んでゆくのだ。

罪悪の深い淵に沈んだ人類の悲惨な状態を憐れんだ神は
人の姿となり　地上に現れ　罪と死からの救いの道を
示されたのだ。主は　人類の心の発達を助ける天使の私にも
早くから新しい使命を付け加えられた。私は日ごと岩山に
張りつけられ　人の心の根源にある傲慢の罪を償い続ける
ことになったのだ。人類の罪は　神の御子イエス・キリスト

の受難によって決定的に償われ　神の愛が　人類を赦し
生かしている。　天使の償いも贖い主キリストの御業の一端を
成している。
それゆえ人類とともにある私は人の姿で現れ　これからも
毎日この岩壁に縛られて　神の正義に打たれるのだ。
見よ。天の高みから正義の天使が現れ　わが身に何をするかを。

　　　　旅の修道士

（独白）　おお　純白の大鷲が光りかがやく雲から現れ　天翔け
舞い降りてきた！　岩壁に張りつけられた天使の頭に　足の
鉤爪を打ちこみ　天使の脇腹を鋭い嘴で引き裂いて　赤黒く
爛れた肝臓を啄んでいる！　受苦の天使が身をよじり　激しい
痙攣で岩が揺れ　轟音が大気を震わせ　山間に谺する！　日が
急にかげり　暗い山肌を冷たい風が吹き抜ける！　死んだ
おお　聖なる天使が　遂にうなだれ動かなくなった。死んだ
天使は　キリストのように甦るのだろうか？

　　　　正義の天使

信仰の薄い人よ。そなたは疑うのか　使命を果たし　自らを
愛の犠牲として奉献した天使の復活を。　人類の罪を負い
死んだ天使は　神に嘉され甦るのだ。この償いの天使は

主キリストの受難に繋がるので　過ぎ越しの浄夜が明ける
たびに復活するのだ。人類とともにいる助力の天使は償いと
甦りによって　人類の精神が働き続けるのを赦されている。
しかし　人間の心は　聖なるものの償いによる赦しを忘れ
たやすく罪の誘惑に陥り　自分の能力を過信して高ぶる。
自力を頼り　真の伴侶である理性を捨てた心は　欲望を
そそる妖艶な傲慢と交わり　罪悪を生み続ける妖魔を
心に囲う。

それゆえ未来の人間は　欲望が駆り立てるままに　快楽を
追い求め　大地の資源を貪り　地球を汚し傷つけるであろう。
延ばし拡げやすい銅や鉄　さらに金銀に目をつけた人間たちは
早くからそれらを含む鉱石を地中から掘り出し　川水で洗い
焚き火で熔かし加工した。それゆえ水と土は汚され　掘った
者たちは　金属の毒で病んだ。未来の人間は　さらに森を
伐り　鉱床を掘りまくり　撒き散らす毒に　人々は病み
苦しむであろう。

また昔から　燃える石や燃える水に目をつけた人間たちは
燃料に用いていたが　未来の人間は　深い地下から黒い石を
掘り出し　黒い水を汲み上げて　それらを燃やした火で
屋内を暖め　金属を熔かし　工作した物を動かすであろう。
太古に埋葬され解体し変容した植物の化石や屍液は　人間の
欲望によって眠りを覚まされ　地上に曝され　焼き尽くされ

炎上する屍炭の妄執の煤煙　屍油の愁嘆の排気は　空を
さまよい覆い　人々を苦しめるであろう。

太陽の熱がこもる大気の体温は上昇し　その中で息をする
生き物はすべて　高温に喘ぐようになるであろう。

原始の森を焼き払った人間たちは　その跡に作物を植えたが
未来の人間は　より多くの利益を求め　土地を休息させず
酷使するであろう。　作物に留まった毒は　人体を蝕み報いるであろう。

土をも侵し弱らせ　水に溶け入り　井戸も池も川も汚す
であろう。　薬を用いて虫を皆殺しにし　毒物は
人間が大量に使い捨てた不溶の毒物も　果てなる海の墓に
入ると　溶解して魚貝に溜まり　食べた人間の体内に帰る
であろう。

森は　伐り倒され　また黒い雨で立ち枯れ　土は流失し
荒れ果てた砂漠が広がるであろう。　清水の沼も川も汚れ
干乾び　鳥も獣も人も命の水に飢え渇くであろう。

多くの生き物の住み処であるさんご礁の森も枯れ果て
白骨林となり　海の華麗な世界は　水底の墓地と化すで
あろう。

地上を傷つけ続ける人間の所業によって　動物　微生物
植物の多くの種が滅び　地球は　健やかで美しい調和を失い
至るところで病める姿を未来の人類に曝すであろう。
自然が病み衰えるとともに　自然の部分を成す人間の
身心も病み衰えるであろう。

世界の病変が進行しても　大地の傷を省みない虚業家は
さらに自然の資源を奪い　巨富を築くために　安値で
買った労力を使い　新奇な品を作り　人々の物欲を
煽って売り出し　巨利を得る。

富を殖やす技術と利益が人の心を奪い　人間は金銭を信じ
拝むようになるであろう。　人々は財貨の奴隷となり
富のお零れにあずかるために走り回る。

昼は日差しで夜は人工灯でかがやく栄華の都　繁栄し
浪費する富める都市の谷底に　貧しい民のぼろ切れの
小屋が止め処なく連なり広がる。

古代から　驕る帝王たちは　民衆の憤懣を静めるために
強国の将来の富を幻想させ　若い者は兵士にして　異国の
豊かな領土を狙い　正義を名目に突き出す槍剣で奪ってきた。

私利を図る悪賢い頭脳が開発し続ける悪魔の乗り物　凶弾を
連射する大小の筒　火を噴き踏みにじる甲鉄の巨象　海を駆け
敵地を打ち叩く鋼鉄の海獣　弾投げ落とす金属の殺戮鳥を
利用して　未来の帝王たちは　地上の領土と資源を狙い
覇権をかけて戦うであろう。

傲り高ぶる頭脳を動員し　遂に権力者たちは　絶滅の超高熱を
生む禁断の弾を完成させ　敵国の大都市の上空で破裂させて
市街と罪無き市民を焼き尽くすであろう。

人間たちは　絶え間ない紛争　内戦　時折の大戦で　殺し

傷つけ合い　　虐殺を逃れた難民は　荒廃した大地を流亡する

であろう。

人類が存亡の危機に瀕しても　強国の権力者たちは

陸海だけでなく　塵覆う空に城まで築き　星の領土と資源を

狙い　天空の専有を画策するであろう。

戦火の治まった時代でも　人間の内なる心の戦いは終わらない

であろう。人間の欲望は鎮まらず燎原（りょうげん）の火であり　未来の

世界を疾走するのは　怪獣が動かす火の車であろう。

この魔性の獣は　金銭を貪り食って肥え太り　欲望の炎を

吹いて　新たに作った金を呑む。

数世紀を駆け抜けるその火車は　生産の前輪と消費の後輪

から成り　留まることなく加速して　野放しにすれば

大地を焼き尽くし　自らを焼き滅ぼすまで止まないであろう。

人力の右輪と機器の左輪から成るその火車は　技術の革新で

左輪ばかりが大きくなり　放任すれば傾いた車は　縺（もつ）りつく

多くの人々を振り落とし　断崖沿いの道を踏み外して

奈落の底に燃え墜ちるであろう。

この危機が人類に迫っても　未来の傲る頭脳は　人手に

代わる人工の知能を作り出し　人間は機器に隷従してゆき

さらに傾き加速する火車は　見えない未来へ向けて盲進する。

自然の命の働きが弱まると　動物や人間の断片から生命を

再生し　種の存続と改良を企て　人は自分の不死の命を

金で買い求めようとするであろう。

死せる神に代わり　生命の創造主になるように呼びかける

魅惑の囁きは　内なる悪魔の声に人は悩まされるであろう。

誘惑に負けた頭脳は　法を犯して禁断の生命の種を操作し

新しい人間の創造を試みるであろう。

これほど人間が罪を犯しても　人類が滅びずに生き続けるのは

主の愛の償いがあり　その御業を日ごと再現する

助力の天使の力添えで　破滅に瀕した人間の心が悔い改めて

正道に立ち返るからなのだ。異国で飢え死にしかけて

改心した放蕩息子が慈父のもとに帰る主の喩え話のように

罪を悔い改めた心は　主に喜ばれ生かされる。

人間の心は　理性を取り戻し　高慢により思考の絡繰り（からくり）に

堕し　人の道を見失っていた頭脳は　賢明な良心に導かれ

謙虚と節制を備えた知性に復位して　知恵の光に照らされ

進むべき道を見渡す。

朝日を浴びる人々は　冷えた化石の心を温かい血肉の心に

変えられる。かれらは滅びの車を降りて　夜明けの世界の

大地を踏み締め　その感触を取り戻し　ゆっくり歩き出す。

かれらは立ち止まり　大地の傷を涙と汗で癒し　大地の病を

同情と労苦で治す。荒地を緑野に変え　甦った草花を愛で
戻ってきた鳥の歌を聴き　大地の恵みの実りを収める。

癒された人々は　かれらと大地の甦りを感謝し　平和と命を
もたらす光を讃える。緑の山々と平野の爽やかな息吹を感じ
地上の人々は　共に喜び　花環を成して踊り歌う。

甦った人々は国境を越え　手を携え　遠い異邦の民は隣人と
なり　貧しい人を助け　弱い人を支えて　世界の民は分かち
合い　真に豊かな世界を目指し　踏み出すであろう。

新しい民は　豊饒な大地を注意深く守り　未来の地上の
生命に忠実に伝え　正義の愛を全うする。

より多くの人々が　愛の世界の実現を目指し　日々の労苦を
捧げて生きる。人々は与えて失わず　かえって富むことを知る。
与えるのは愛であるゆえ。
しかし万人がそれを知って行うわけではない。暗闇の軍勢は
旅する民さえも襲うであろう。それゆえ地上の人間は　世の
終わりまで　闇の勢力と戦い続けるであろう。
主の愛の掟を守り　愛の防具を身に帯びる者のみが　戦いに
打ち勝つであろう。

神は　ご自身を譲り与える愛によって宇宙を創造し　無限の
愛の御業で統べ給う。
それゆえ万象は　続く現象に場を譲る。それらは　主から
受けた内なる愛の本性に従い　自己を超越し　大いなる愛の
世界に入り働く。極微の物質も無心の愛で宇宙に流転する。
愛は　自己の存在を譲り与えることであり　万象が関わり
合う宇宙の不変の原理なのだ。

　　　　　旅の修道士

主キリストが　すべての人を救うために　罪を償う犠牲
として　ご自身の奉献を続けられ　その尊い仲介によって
人類が赦され生き続けていることを改めて知りました。
また未来の人々が救われるためには　高慢と貪欲の罪を
悔い改め　理性を取り戻して欲望を抑え　節制によって
知足の生活に立ち返り　周囲の世界と和して共に生きる
必要があることも知りました。
創造主の御心による宇宙の真理が　万物の自己譲与の
愛にあることも悟りました。
それでも人類の罪を超えて　時に人間を激しく撃つ悪から
どのように人間は救われるのでしょうか？
なにゆえ　度重なる地震　津波　噴火などの大災害によって
罪の無い人々が苦しめられるのですか？

正義の天使

自然の激動は　人間の眼から見れば災禍の悪であるが
創造主の眼には災禍ではなく　生きる地球の律動であり
その力の放出なのだ。人間は与えられた知性を可能な限り
働かせて　その激動に対処するべきであり　それらを
生の試練として認めるべきなのだ。
生きている地球の激動を恨み嘆いてはならない。主の
愛の内に息づく大自然の変調から生命が誕生したのだから。
あらゆる存在は　宇宙の律動　形成と崩壊　生と死の流転の
中で変動している。古い存在は朽ち失せ　新しい存在が
形を成し甦る。この存在の生死の律動は　より高い存在への
前進なのだ。
愛によって存在を与えられたものは　苦しみをも与えられる。
存在の苦しみは　より高い存在の歓喜へ向かうから。
崩壊し滅びゆく古い存在は　存在の新生を予感し
存在の苦しみは　新生の歓喜の光に溶け入るであろう。

私は知っている。地上の人々の生活　病　老い　死の
苦しみを。生きる苦しみから逃げてはならない。
人は苦しみによって知恵を学ぶのだ。
苦しみを厭わしい生の罰の重荷とするか　光明への忍耐の

証しとするかは　その人の自由な意志に委ねられている。
できれば苦しみを主への奉献と成して　主への信仰と生の
希望を強めるがよい。
耐えられぬほど苦しいときは　神に寄り縋るがよい。
苦しむ人の内なる神は　肩代わりして苦しみを取り除き
人は安らぎを得るであろう。
最も大きい苦しみも　人が耐えられぬものではない。
苦しみに耐えよ。苦しみを受け入れ　その火に心身を
投じ入れよ。慈愛の主の試煉は　耐えられる道　光明へ
の道なのだ。
主の激しい愛の焔は　苦しむ人の心を浄め鍛え
その心は精錬されて　復活の歓喜に生きるであろう。
私が言うまでもなく　キリストに従う人は知っている筈だ。
この苦しみと死の過ぎ越しの道が　不滅の生命へ至る
道であるのを。

宇宙に生滅する存在の苦しみからすべての存在を救うために
神は愛する御子を宇宙にお与えになり　受肉したキリストは
身をもって苦しみを体現し　全人類だけでなく　宇宙の
すべての存在に救いの道を示されたのだ。
キリストの十字架は　宇宙の中心の指標なのだ。
宇宙のあらゆる存在は　十字架の苦しみと死を過ぎ越して
新生の歓喜に至るゆえ。見よ。この岩山の頂上を。

(25)

(天空からの光が暗い山頂を照らし出し、円光の包む十字架に張りつけられたキリストの像が現れる)

旅の修道士

(独白)　おお　何と痛ましいお姿！　茨の冠で血まみれの頭をうなだれ　お体の重みで釘づけされた両手足は破れ裂け危うく全身を吊るしている。苦しみ喘ぐお体は　血の汗を噴いている。

人類のすべての罪を一身に負い　世界のすべての苦しみを担い　苦しんでおられるのだ。

真昼なのに地平の果てまで暗くなってきた！　主のお体は動かない。十字架上の死によって　すべての悪に打ち勝ちご自身を尊い犠牲として父なる神に捧げておられるのだ。

この無限の愛の奉献によって　すべての存在を悪から救われているのだ。

(一瞬閃く槍の穂先がキリストの脇腹を突き刺し、血と水が噴き出て地にしたたる。修道士は、ひれ伏して祈り続ける。深い祈りの後、彼は再び山頂と岩壁を見上げる)

頂上に光っていた十字架のキリストの御像が消えている！

澄み切った青空しか見えない。岩に縛られていた助力の天使も　傍らの大鷲の天使も消えている！岩壁は日光を浴びて褐色にかがやき静まり返っている。

私が今まで見たのは　白昼の夢か幻か。

(修道士は山路を少し戻り、洞窟を再び覗く)

おや　老人の姿が見えない。奥に老人の被っていた白布と敷いていた筵がたたんで置いてある。神のご加護によって病の激痛の責め苦から解放され　この岩山を下りて行ったのだろう。

今こそ私は知る。この岩山が私の聖地となったのを。聖地は名高い巡礼の地に限らない。聖地は至る所にあるのだ。神が人の心を訪れるとき　心が聖所となり　心の聖地となるからだ。

私の心の聖地が悪に汚されず　変わらぬ聖所であり続けますように。

ああ　うねる山々　大きい谷間　青い樹海　緑の草原散在する村々　すべてが明るい光を浴びて安らかに息づいている。眼の前の光あふれる平和な風景が私の魂の平和な光景であり続けますように。

地平まで広がる大高原のはるか彼方に　アララト山が
白くかがやいている。町のどのような大聖堂にもまして
天地を荘厳する壮麗な自然の大聖堂　巡礼たちの
はるかな旅路を示す聖なる道標だ。
目指す平原はまだ遠い。
さあ　日が暮れる前に　山麓の修道院に辿り着き
一晩泊めてもらうために　早く峠の山路を下りて行こう。

劇詩　世阿弥

登場人物　　旅の男
　　　　　　土地の老人
　　　　　　世阿弥の霊

場所　　　　佐渡島

時代　　　　二十世紀末のある年の初秋

第一場　七浦海岸

（リュックサックと寝袋を背負う旅の男が海辺の道に現れる）

旅の男

この奇岩怪石の続く海岸の荒磯に立つと　何と心地良いことか。
岩を襲い嚙む険しい歯牙の白波に　卑小な己も打ち砕かれ
はるばると波濤を越えた冷たい潮風が　絶えず私を吹き抜け
身も心も透き通り　雑念の水泡の消える無我の境地に入った
ようだ。

おや　岩場の中に人がいる。引き潮の岩礁で遊んでいるのか。
何かを手にして上がってくるようだ。

（魚籠と鉤を持つ漁師風の老人が現れる）

土地の老人

今日はおとなしい空ですのう。わしになんか用事かなあ。

(30)

旅の男

こんにちは。別に用ではなくて　ただ打ち寄せる白波と広い岩場が面白くて見ていたのです。ここで何が捕れるのですか？

土地の老人

ここじゃ冬は　岩のり長藻に銀葉藻　春は　若布やおさが採れるっちゃ。　夏は　もずくに岩がぎ　さぜえや蛸は年から年中さ。

旅の男

ここは豊かな漁場なんですね。でもこんな岩場で危なくないですか？　随分お年のようですが。

土地の老人

なに慣れとるが。こりゃ磯遊びでねぇ。これで口に食うとるでなあ。お前さんは旅もんやなあ。そげえに荷を負うてどこから来たかや？

旅の男

新潟から船で両津（りょうつ）に渡り　山小屋泊りで山地を越え　外海府（そとかいふ）の入埼（にゅうざき）に下りて　キャンプ場に泊まり　海沿いに歩いたりバスに乗ったりして　相川の古い町並みを抜け　この七浦海岸（ななうら）まで来たのです。

土地の老人

そりゃ大層な旅じゃ。そいで今日はどこへ行きなさる？

旅の男

ここで足を休めた後　台ヶ鼻の岬を回って佐和田に行き　今日はキャンプ場に貸しテントを張って泊まる積もりです。

土地の老人

足まめな御仁じゃなあ。わしも捕れた貝を橘の岬の旅館に届けて帰るので　途中まで行くかね。橘から佐和田までのバスもあるけに。

旅の男

それは良いですね。ご一緒しましょう。

（二人は浜の上の道路に上がり、老人は道端の荷車の生け簀に
魚籠の貝を移す）

土地の老人

その背中の荷物はきついじゃろ。車の後ろは空いとるので荷物を
置いたらええ。

旅の男

ありがとうございます。その代わり私も梶を持ちましょう。

（二人は並んで梶を持ち、荷車を引き始める）

こんなにせっせと働いておられるとは　お年に負けず
お元気ですね。

土地の老人

年とっても心と体は使わにゃならん。年寄りは足から弱るので
わしはなるだけ体を使い　車に頼らんで歩く。中休みしちゃ
働くもんが楽しう余生するっちゃ。
お前さんもよう歩かっしゃるが　都会の人かや？

旅の男

私は東京から来ました。若いころから山歩きをしていたので
歩くのは慣れています。飲み物を製造する会社に勤めていた
ので　実益を兼ねて山旅では　山の泉や渓谷の水質を調べて
いたのです。
ところがこの不景気で　長年勤めていた会社がつぶれて
失業したので　この度は身の振り方を考える旅になりました。

土地の老人

そりゃ大事じゃなあ。屋根から屋根石が落ちてくるような
もんよ。それであんたは気楽な独り身かね？

旅の男

いいえ　家内も会社で働いていて　大学三年生の息子と
高校二年生の娘がいます。家内は契約社員で給料は安く

身分も不安定ですし　私が無職になったので　家族は
先行きの生活不安に怯えています。この酷い不景気で
息子は将来就職できないのを恐れているし　娘は
進学するか就職するかで悩んでいます。

それでも四十代の峠を越えて失業したのを転機に
自分の半生を振り返り　これから家族とともに
生きる道を探るために　独り旅に出て
このように佐渡の地を歩き続けているのです。

会社に勤めているときは　朝晩満員の電車に乗って
郊外の自宅と都心のオフィスの間を往復して　大都会の
人混みと騒音にも馴らされていましたが　この佐渡の
旅で　巨大の原生林を抜け　山の尾根を辿り　野原に
咲き静まる花々　谷川の岩清水　真っ青な大海原　荒磯に
寄せ来る白い波濤に　身を置いているうちに　私の中の
原始の感覚がよみがえり　根本に立ち返って生きる活力も
目覚めてきた感じがするのです。

　　　　土地の老人

そりゃえことよ。　都会から離れた海山にゃ人を直す力が
あるっちゃ。　大都会は　人の心も命も食いもんにする
恐ろしい所や。　銭の力が渦のごと何もかも引き寄せ
吸いこんでしまう恐ろしい所よ。

あの戦争で　兵隊に取られ　外地へ遣られた多くの若衆が
島に帰って来れんかった。　運気の良いわしは　戦地で
殺されんで　終戦で島に戻った後　網元に雇われて
沖で漁をしとった。　そのうち嫁さんをもろうて　男の子と
娘っ子も生まれたっちゃ。

せがれが高校を出て漁師になったとき　漁協から借金して
小型の船を買い　親子で沖に出て漁に精を出したもんよ。
それも長う続かんかった。台風で船がひどう壊れてしもうて
漁がでけんごとなったんや。

せがれは　労賃の安い雇いの漁師にゃならん　借金を
済ませて船をまた買うには　都会で働いて金を貯める方が
早いと言い張って　東京に出稼ぎに行ったんよ。

一年後に橋桁工事の現場の事故で死んでしもうた。
急なことにも死に目にも会えんやった。　都会に出したせえで
せがれを若ざかりで殺してしもうた。

娘が嫁いで新潟に行ってから　夫婦だけの暮らしになって
二人で磯に行ちゃ藻草や貝を取ってたよ。

母さんは働きもんで　浜のもんやから　秋の取り入れの
時になりゃ　国中に泊まりで出かけて働いとった。
裏の畑で野菜も少し作って　お蔭で二人の口が干上がる
ことはなかったさ。

それがあれほど元気もんやったのに　五年前に病にかかり

寝返りも打てんほど痛がって　食いもんも口に入れんで
痩せ細り　とうとう先立たれてしもうた。わしの長年の
連れ添いも命しもうて　沖の向こうに一人で行ってしもうたよ。
もう帰らんけに　ほんまに寂しゅうなった。それからは
ずっと独り暮らしで　娘が心配して　新潟に来んかと
言うてくれるが　この暮らしが気楽で　まだ元気なので
こうして働いとるっちゃ。

そいでも寂しゅうなったのは　わしの家だけやない。若衆が島を
離れて行き　田畑を作るもんも　魚を捕るもんも年寄りばかりで
若いもんは継がん。

村はどこも人が減ってしまうて　島を回る広い道が通って
大きなフェリーが運んでくるてしもうたけど　島の定期バスは
すっかり減って　村の年寄りにゃ不便になった。

道が良うなって　七浦に夕日を見に来る旅もんが増え　岬の
旅館が賑わうのはええけど　旅もんは増えても　佐渡もんが
減って　生きとるもんも死んでゆけば　島はどうなるんやろう？
元より米も野菜もよう取れ　魚もよう捕れる島で　野山に
出りゃ花もよう咲いて　ゆるりと暮らせる所やから
若いもんが銭にまさるその魅力に気づいて　島に居てくれりゃ
いいに。そいでも人が減るんやったら　あんたのような
都会のもんが　どんどん島に移り住んでくれたら　みんなが
豊かに生きられるんやがなあ。

さて長手の岬も近うなった。あんたは橘から佐和田にバスで
行ったらええ。まだ最終の便があるやろ。台ヶ鼻を回りゃ
入り海になって　その向こうに見えるのが佐和田の越の
松原よ。

昔流人の法師がその松林の庵に住んどったという言い伝えを
わしがまだ小さいとき　じいさんから聞いたことがある。
佐和田の先の真野は　昔の流人が多く住んどった土地やから
跡を訪うて偲んだら　ええ供養になるやろ。

ここまで車を引いてくれて大きに。わしは岬の旅館に
これを届けて帰るが。

　　　　　　　　　　　　旅の男

とても為になるお話を聞かせて頂いて　ありがとうございます。
この旅での一期一会のひとときは　生涯忘れ難いものに
なるでしょう。私はここで失礼します。佐和田にはバスで
行きますよ。それでは　いつまでもお元気で。さようなら。

　　　　　　　土地の老人

あんたもこの旅で運気が開けるとええなあ。そいじゃ元気に
旅を続けなされ。さようなら。

第二場　佐和田の松林　テントの中

（旅の男はキャンプ場に張った貸しテントの中で簡単な夕食を
済ませた後、しばらく休息する）

　　　　　旅の男

（独白）　何と静かな夕暮れだろう。ときどき聞こえる砂浜の
波の音も　松風の音も　心を静めてくれる。日が落ちて
涼しくなった林の草むらから　鈴虫も鳴き始めた。夕闇が
迫っているが　この二畳ほどの草地の明かりとしては
受け皿に立てた一本のろうそくの炎で足りる。
この幽境に居ると　自宅から遠く離れた地にありながら
自室で安座し　本来の自己に帰っている心地がする。
さて　茶を点てるためにコッヘルで湯を沸かそう。この水は
今朝発ったとき　村の農家に立ち寄り　井戸の清水を乞い
瓶に汲み入れ運んできたもの。
職を失って　これから生きる道を求めて旅する私が
遠い昔から多くの流人が住んだというこの地に一夜宿り
遠流の古人をしみじみと偲ぶのも何かの縁であろう。
七浦海岸で出会い　道連れになったあの老人が話していた

ように　この松林のどこかに昔流人の法師が庵を結んでいた
のであれば　今宵供える茶は　その清風心空の修行者に
手向けるのがふさわしいだろう。
このコップを花筒として　林で摘んだ一輪の野菊を活け
この小皿を香炉として　一抹の香を焚こう。
丁度よく湯が沸いてきた。この清らかな湯で茶を点てて
法師の霊に一碗を捧げよう。

（献茶に続いて茶を点て飲んだ後、旅の男は灯りを消し、
拡げた寝袋にくるまって眠る。深夜に目を覚ました男は、
テントの中が明るいのに気づいて起き上がる）

　　　　　旅の男

この明るさはどうしたことだろう。明け方の光ではない
ようだ。まだ夜更けなのに　小窓から射しこむ月光で
こんなに明るいのだ。

（男はテントの出入り口を開けて外を見る）

天空に満月がかかり　松の梢から漏れる冴えた光に　林が
白く浮かび　草陰の虫たちが声を惜しまず鳴き交わしている。
草の夜露は白く光を放っている。すぐ近くの空き地は

月に隈なく照らされ　ひときわ明るいようだ。
こんな夜に　月の光に身を浸さないのは惜しいことだ。

（男は上衣を着て外に出る）

第三場　松林の空き地

（空き地に近づいた男は、隅の古いベンチに座って月光を浴びて
いる）

　　　　　旅の男

こんな冷える夜更けの林の中に。この近くの方ですか？
もしもし　どうしてそこに立っているのですか？
空き地の月光の中に人が佇んでいるようだ。
白衣の中に　人影のようなものが透いて見える。
いや　白い薄衣が月の光を浴びて　さらに白く光っているのだ。
立ちこめているのか。
あれ　空き地の真中が特に明るいようだ。白い霧が滞り

　　　　　世阿弥の霊

木陰から呼びかけるのは　この松林に宿ると覚しき旅の御人か。
人界に降りた今は何を隠そう。われは　いにしえの室町の代に
有り難き生を受け　能芸を習い徹した世阿弥の霊である。
先ほど　天の光明界に　白菊の花の下より現れ　色とりどりの

無尽の天華に加わり　清き香りがほのぼの匂い　焚く香の
芳ばしき香りも下より立ち昇り　天上界の名香に交わり馥郁（ふくいく）と
匂い満ちて　群れる天人天女の衣にも染み　また清けき
茶湯は　霊泉より沸沸と湧き出で　われは飛天の皆とともに
神泉に寄り　妙なる法味の甘露にて　喉（のど）潤わせ舞いたった。

神仏への供養の心尊く喜ばしと　舞いつつ下界を見れば
何と　わが生前過ごした黄金の島の松林より　手向けの香花
茶湯の香りが　かすかに一条立ち昇るのを見た。
かつて　その島に仮住みし　この松林の草の庵で　座禅を行じ
神仏故人に香花を献じ　茶を供えたのを思い出し　数多の
世々を隔てた今の世に　われをも供養し給うかと訝しみ（いぶか）
その御人に回向し報いるために　この懐かしき金島の
円月照らす松の林に　天上界より舞い降りたのだ。

　　　　　旅の男

（傍白）おお　何という不思議なことか！　遠い昔の
名高い人が　不意に現れ　この私に話しかけてくるとは！
（世阿弥の霊に）仰せの通り　松林に宿る旅の者です。
あなた様が　その昔この島に流されたのは　書物で知って
いましたが　今宵手向けた法師こそ　その御方とは
思い及ばず　私の至らぬ心をお赦しください。
遠い代に流人の法師が松林に庵していたという言い伝えを

聞き　その法師を偲んで　今宵林の天幕の中で　ささやかな
香花を捧げ　一碗の粗茶を手向けたまでです。
それに私自身が職を失い　寄る辺ない身で　道を尋ねて
さまよい歩いているので　とりわけ遠流の法師が　いかに
配所で修行されたのかを思い　その聖の求道の跡を探る心を
含めて供養したのです。

　　　　　世阿弥の霊

故人への供養は　その人の冥福を祈ることゆえ　その福利は
増すといえども　供養の心広くあらば　天上の群れ皆　福楽を
得る。無辺の仏心は冥途の亡者をも救うという。仏道を慕い
求める人は　広く衆生済度の心もて供養すべきである。
神仏は供養する人の物ではなく心を受けるゆえ　心の供養こそ
嘉（か）せらるる。長者の万灯より貧者の一灯と古き経に言う。
真心の一灯が天上の光をいや増すのを天人たちは歓喜（かんぎ）する。
供養は自身の内なる仏性（ぶっしょう）の働きにして　その極まりは仏果の
悟りに入ることなれば　必ず供養は求道の部分を成す。
おんみがわが道を尋ねるのであれば　おんみに回向し
われが生前に辿った道を語ろう。

旅の男

あなた様の尊い功徳の回向を賜り　まことに畏れ多く
ありがとうございます。かかる不思議なことも仏縁と信じ
謹んでお話を承ります

世阿弥の霊

およそ修行は　僧堂庵室での勤行に限らず　行住坐臥の
すべてに及び　さらに在家出家の別なく　生そのものが
学道である。

生前に能芸を習い工夫していたわれも　その芸が求道に
他ならぬと年長けてようやく知ったのだ。
われは　幼きころより父の傍らにて自然に能を学び
常に父を見習い　その心と技を受け継ぎ　この芸の道を
究めようと一生修行したのだ。

父なる観阿弥は　大和の国の山田に生まれ　能役者となり
結埼に一座を立て　申楽の位を上げようと精進された。
すぐれて世に合い流行りたる田楽の一忠を師と仰ぎ
その芸の風体に学び　また申楽の小歌の節に　曲舞の
拍子を加え　面白き音曲に改め　それが広まり観世の節と
世に聞こえるに至り　一座は京に上りて　こなたかなたの

寺社にて行い　やがて醍醐寺にて七日つかまつり　観世は
申楽の達人よと天下の名望を得たのだ。
童のわれも舞台に立ちて　まことに上手と称えられた。
京の今熊野の申楽に　将軍家お成りの時より　父子とも
ひいきにされて　いよいよ観世座の名は上がった。

われは都の貴人に愛されたが　姿形うるわしく時めく春の花は
真の花にあらず　ただ時分の花とわきまえ　よく身を慎み
能の技を大事にし　声爽やかに謡い　舞の一一の型も確と
身に付くように稽古した。
若き為手は　十七八より声変わり体も変わり　初めの花散り
失すれば　己が立ち舞のおかしく見ゆる姿を恥じ　意気を失い
心腐りて　能止まる危ふき時の至るは必定。
この頃　われは心中に願を立て　生涯能を捨てぬと誓う心を
起こし　稽古の基を守り　無理に強いず声を使い　内々に
稽古を続けていた。

折しも父は　駿河浅間神社にて能を奉納した後　その地にて
五十二で身罷り　若年のわれが観世座の棟梁を継ぐことと
なったのだ。

旅の男

申楽座が多く競い合っていた時代に　まだ若くして

座を継いで　随分難儀をされたこととお察しいたします。
いかにして　その苦しい時を凌がれたのですか？

　　　　世阿弥の霊

父亡き後に座を継いだわれの負いたる荷は重く　先途の
難儀を思い胸潰れたが　年々の大和の社寺のご神事には
大和のゆかりある座の助けを得て勤めを果たし　また
京にて他の座と競わずに　もっぱら遠国田舎を廻り
鄙人（ひなびと）の楽しむ興行をなし　われらの身を助けたのだ。
亡父の遺戒ありがたく　一座の衆は同心しわれを守り立て
わが新しき風体の現るるを気長く待った。かくて二四五で
声直り体も定まり　心を入れて稽古に励んだ。

およそ芸を極めたる達人となるためには　努めて芸の境を拡げ
芸の位を上げるべきである。この芸の正道を達人なりし父の
芸より学んだ。
わが能芸の境を拡げるために　当代の天下に名望ありし
近江申楽の犬王より優美なる歌舞の風体を学び　後に
田楽能の増阿弥からは　冷えたる能の風情を学び　虚心に
おのれの芸風を深めたのだ。
また父が大事にしたように　遠国辺地をもしばしば訪れ
田舎人の心にかなう芸をした。　都を離れて度かさなる旅の

空にて知ったのだ。貴賤上下を選ばず　万人の心を映す
明鏡が　至れる芸の境地であると。
さらに物真似の数を尽くし　あらゆる風体を身につけて
漏れたる所なき芸の達人となるべく稽古を積んだ。
また過ぎたる時分のおのれの風姿を忘れず　今に含み持ち
万事にわたる為手になろうと心がけ　わが芸を拡げたのだ。

されども芸の境地は　それにて終わらず。すべて芸には
上下の位があるゆえ。仏道を極めたる僧を聖と讃え敬う
ように　芸の道を極めたる妙絶の達人を芸の聖と讃え
人は敬う。悟りに達し妙覚の位に至れる菩薩が　衆生を救い
光明へ導くように　芸の妙位を極めたる聖の芸は　その妙用
により　衆人の心を楽しませつつ　智慧へ導く。
芸道は仏道修行をまねる求道であり　上智の芸に　かくも
尊き用あれば　芸人も作者も　至境妙花の芸に至るべく
芸の向上に努めるべきである。
われも年盛りに　大和補巌寺（ふがんじ）の住持より禅を学んだ後
京の五山に師家（しけ）の教示を頂き　くり返し禅話語録を味わい
禅法をもって　わが能芸の道を究めようと一途に工夫し
精進したのだ。

されど当代の芸人の有り様を見るに　芸の妙花の悟道を辿らず
芸の修行も疎かに　世の常に習い一夕（いっせき）の喝采　一日の評判を

求め　心なき能を早まり見せる者が多かった。
時分の花を得たる上手も名利に染まり　心驕りて初心を忘れ
工夫を極めず　妙花の芸位に上がらず　能下がりて　この芸の
達人は世に稀であった。大方は能の真実を知らず　正しき
修行を身につけず　無明の闇にさまよっていた。
遡るべき源泉に養われざる芸の命は　末技に痩せ細り
枯れ落ちて朽ち果てるのみ。この芸道もはや末期に至り
衰え滅びゆくかと憂えて　道のため　われは跡継ぎに伝えて
おくべく　能の奥義をさまざまに書き記したのだ。

われは時の花をかざさず　生涯修行の心もて至芸の妙位を求め
わが芸を好み　能の知見を尋ぬる目利の貴人も居給えば
定めなき浮世にあれども　時流に節を曲げず　亡父の伝えたる
家風を保っていた。
嫡男元雅も能芸に精進し　優れたる為手にして作能にも秀で
年盛りに向かい名人の器量を見せれば　安心して子に観世の
大夫（たゆう）を継がせ　出家せるわれは座を後見し　能芸の伝授に
心を砕いた。

かくて寒風吹きすさぶ冬が来たのだ。
新しき室町殿は執心深き人にて　芸にも及ぶまつりごとの
力を天下に見せんとてか　われら父子が仙洞御所に参内し
上皇様お望みの能つかまつる用意をさし止めた。

さらにわが務めたる醍醐寺清滝宮の楽頭の職を解き
将軍家ごひいきの音阿弥に替えた。
座中の太鼓役ながら作能の才をも見せたる次男元能は
京での興行を禁ぜられた座の行く末をはかなみ　わが日頃の
芸談を取りまとめた後　憂き世を逃れ出家した。
その後二年を経ずして　大夫を継げる元雅が　興行で
田舎へ下り　伊勢の国を廻っていた折　安濃の津にて
身罷ったという急事を知らせる便りが届いたのだ。

寿天は天命にして　老少不定の生死なれども
わが子にわかに先立ち逝けば　まったく思いの外なる心地して
前途ある子の無念を思い　暗夜の涙衣をうるおし　悲嘆のあまり
老残の身は弱り　心の闇に臥し沈めば　心身ともに朽ち果てる
思いで　夜陰の鐘も　わが死出を弔う鐘の音かと覚えた。
子ながらも類いなき達人となり　この道を継げる息男に
わがことごとく記し伝えたる芸道の奥義秘伝は　一時の夢幻
泡影　無益の塵煙と消え失せるのみ。
元雅の早世によって　当流の道は絶え　一座はすでに破滅した。
わがあさましき老命のみ残って　今となりかかる憂き目に
遭うとは　悲しみに堪えず。何と哀れな老いの身よ。

　　旅の男

（傍白）　おお　いとも尊き天人の怪しき有り様！
薄衣に透く人影の身は激しく波打ち　うつ伏せる顔に
衣の袖を当てている！　秋の夜を照らす明月も
雲に隠れてしまった！　肌寒い松風がにわかに吹き荒れ
木立が悲鳴をあげて揺れている。

　　　　　世阿弥の霊

火車に運ばれ　炎噴き上げ　転び廻るぞ無残なる。

（傍白）　天人が変化して　吹き募る嵐に身をまかせ
緋色に変じた衣をなびかせ　笹の葉を手に髪振り乱し
怨霊の鬼の面懸け　空き地を駆け廻り　狂い舞っている！

　　　　　　旅の男

心は愛着の網に捕らわれ　煩悩の犬畜生と化し　妄執の
思い出があまりにも切なれば　たちまち身内によみがえり

　　　　　世阿弥の霊

極熱の業苦を受けて　狂い廻り　阿鼻の地獄に舞い墜つるなり。
踏む露草は野火と焼け　縋りつく木は火柱となり
闇に惑う心の行方は風すさび　燃える炎を身にまとい

（天人は激しい動きを止めて、面を伏せる）

座禅して静かに観じ　心の平安を得たり。
老心の妄執は末期の一大事の障りになるばかりと懺悔し
清涼の風と化して吹けば　身も爽やかに生き返る心地して
心は我にかえり　おのれを省みて　地獄の猛火　たちまち
捨て給わず。　魔道にさえ　阿弥陀の光明さし込めば　はっと
それ仏の円光は　十方世界を遍照し　念仏の衆生を摂取して

　　　　　　旅の男

（傍白）　今は直面の慈顔の天人が　静かに白衣を拡げ
舞っている。　何と妙なる幽玄な姿！　黒い嵐は過ぎ去り
海波も静まり　澄みきった天空の満月が皎々とかがやき
涼しい夜風の松林を静寂に照らしている！　清らかな
月光の中　天人は舞い納めて立っている。

　　　　　世阿弥の霊

芸道の花散り失せても　その種を後代の人の心が受け保たば
神仏の計らいにより　いつの世にか芸の命は甦り　花も豊かに
咲き匂うであろう。　おのれを離れた芸道は神慮仏智に任すべし。

我が家の芸道絶えたるを嘆き　日夜を空しく過ごして何の功があろう。余命推し量るほどに老いたる今　最も大事なる道を行ぜずして　あたら時光を失うは悔しきことなり。芸の道絶え　心は繋縛を解いた今　一寸の光陰を惜しみ　芸に依らざる修行を始めるべきと　われは初心に帰り　仏道を学び始めた。

それゆえ息男の身罷りて二年を経ずして　何事の咎にやあらん　室町殿より佐渡への配流の沙汰ありし折　半よ世を捨てたる身なれば　逆境を恨まず　平常心を失わず　行雲流水に身を託す心地で　遠流の島へ旅立ったのだ。

若狭の小浜より船路となり　遥かに雪の白山を仰ぎ　能登の長き海辺にも移ろい　珠州の岬も過ぎて　闇のかなたの漁り火を後に　明けゆく天の立山を拝み　やがて佐渡の大田の浦に着いた。明けて山路を上り下りて　その夜ようやく配所の新保なる地に着き　小寺を仮の宿とした。

しかるに島にも戦起こりて　配所に戦火が及び　西に逃れて泉なる地の寺に宿を移した。ようやく侘び住まいに慣れ　地頭殿の計らいで外に出づるは自在なれば　近辺の寺社旧跡にも参り　日々の心を慰めた。

ある時は　宿の近くの草原が　順徳院の御所の跡と聞き訪ねてみた。秋の日の寂しき原は　黒木の御所の柱も朽ち失せ

ただ草茫々と生い茂り　草葉の蔭の虫の声も弱りて　啾啾と吹き渡る秋風の中　昔遷されし帝の痛ましき身の上を偲んだ。

風吹き通す荒屋に独り坐し　帝は都をつゆも忘れず　御衣の袂を濡らし給うたのか。泉の清水に明月の映るごとく　帝の御心が澄み透ったのであれば　日々の奈落の火焔の道も涼しき悟りの道と変化し　荒ぶる御心も静まり安んじ　苦患の憂き世を逃れ給うたであろう。

またある時は遠出して　寺の様子も風光も　大和の長谷寺によく似たる　名だたる御仏を拝み　長谷寺と申す古き山寺に詣で　時折この霊地にも参るようになった。

心細き遠き国にも社寺多く　神仏身近にましませば　崇め敬う舞を手向けて　白雲万波のはるか隔てて　嘆く家人の息災安穏を祈願した。

遠国にてのわが小謡や小舞を見たる国人も居て　指南を乞える幾人かに謡と舞を折々教えた。諸人は謝金か畑物を届け　さらに入り江の松林の荒れ果てたる空き小屋を直し　庵に変えてわれに贈った。

かくて歳月の茫々と流れるままに　泉の寺の仏堂で

また松の林の草庵で　われは坐禅を行じ　四方の寺社に参詣し
風情ある地で　神仏に舞を奉献し続けたのだ。

（しばらく沈黙した天人は、軽く足拍子を踏み、松の小枝を
持つ右手を前方に差し出して廻す）

旅の男

（傍白）おお　天人が静かにゆっくり舞い始める！　追憶の
内にあっても　歌舞の不滅の力は天人をも動かすのか。

世阿弥の霊

（序の舞を荘重に舞いつつ謡い始める）

春のあけぼの　山際の空明けゆけば　金色の雲たなびきて
広き遠野に　白霞立ち　雪解けの水光きらめくせせらぎの
流れ清けき声を謡に　山越えわたる朝風を笛の音として
若草萌える地にそそぐ春の光に　天道供養の舞を奉じた。

鰭魚(はたうお)恵む神仏に　沖の漁りの無事祈り　風を鎮める舞を捧げた。

遠山に　花の雲の霞かかれば　花に誘われ　心浮き
急ぎ出で立ち　山路分け入り　風に散り舞う花の光に
万象の心を観じ　野辺に咲き散りゆく花を惜しめども
心より心に映る面影の光の花こそ　常住不滅の花と知り
われは空の桜の精となり　山渡り花吹き散らす嵐を笛に
行方を知らず　無常安穏　転身歓喜　仏法散華の舞を舞った。

行く春を惜しみ送るも　今は限りと心がけ　風薫り
花咲きすさぶ野にも出で　色とりどりの花と語らい
光さす青葉若葉の林に入れば　ほしいまま鳴く山鳥を
笛と鼓に　谷川の高鳴る音を謡とし　精爽やかな社で舞い
風そよぐ植田に立ちて　黄金の瑞穂の実りを祈り　遠田の
蛙の天にも届く声を謡に　望み見る満目青山を讃えて舞った。

光り輝く夏の日は　涼求め　陰懐かしみ　万緑映ゆる
社に詣で　初立ちの若き女夫の参るを見かけ　歳古りて
奇すしき杉の緑陰に立ち　榊葉を手に　光降る　島の社に
神いまし　万象結ぶ　御業讃えよと　神を言祝(ことほ)ぐ舞を奉じた。

春麗らかな一日は　海辺に行きて　白波寄せる荒磯に立ち
魚群れる早潮望み　轟き響む海鳴りを　龍神うなる謡とし
岩壁を打つ怒濤を鼓に　海の涯より照り渡る光に向かい

暑き日は　夏草静む原を越え　海山望む岡にも上り
心地よき風の立ち来る海の果て　白山権現の神の光の

影向に立つ　金北山の光背を成し　輝く雲の峰を見上げて
天に描ける荘厳の霊威の山を遥拝し　神に手向けの舞を捧げた。

声を笛とし　山寺の入相の鐘の音を鼓に　回向の舞を供養した。

昔の人気なきみささぎに参り　夕べの篝のはかなく
ゆらめく炎を明かりに　暗き社の奥処に隠れ　哭く啄木鳥の

秋の初風肌寒く　物思う頃　ひぐらしの鳴く林を辿り

天高く澄み渡る日の夕べには　中秋の明月を見んと
御崎の浜に遠く行き　入り日の沈む海の彼方の寂光に
西方浄土を祈願して舞い　夜に入れば　天空かかる満月の
波も静まる海に照り映え　渺茫寂静の光の海に　万象還り
寄せては返る波を拍子に　光明遍照　法楽悦惚の舞を奉じた。

秋深まれば　空渡る鳥を見送り　野の露草の光を惜しみ
深く色づく山に入り　照り映える炎の紅葉　静かに散り落ち
埋む落葉の地に輝けば　万象の変化流転に　神仏の光影を観じ
鳥の声　谷水の音に　山水の説法を聴き　妙法讃歎の舞を舞った。

冬の来て　嵐のあとの一日は　枯れ立ちの林にも入り
茨の朱実に冬深き光を捉え　山鳥の光幽けき影も移ろい
朽ち葉埋まる枯れ谷の寂静の内　滅びしものの輝き増せば
目眩むほどの光に包まれ　寂滅光耀　新生凝望の舞を捧げた。

新しき年の始めは　暁に起き　若水を汲み　清々しき朝
白雪映える社に詣でて　四海静穏　衆生浄福を祈って舞った。
風霜に耐える巌に花咲くごとく　老骨に心の花のなお在れば
命の限り万象を祝い　神仏を讃えることこそ　老いの本意なれ。

厳冬の下界静まる極寒の夜　物を離れ　我を
離れて　雪の明かりの凍原に立ち　冴えまさる銀河を仰ぎ
ほのかに瞬く群星の声明を謡に　天界の妙なる調べを音曲に
黙照の天の広座に進み出で　妙境現成　光明歓喜の舞を奉じた。

（天人は法悦の状態で舞い終えると、しばらく沈黙した後、
静かに語り始める）

かくのごと　遊山法楽の舞を舞い続け　われがこの地に
至れるは　芸を究め　生を全うする道を供え給える神仏の
御心と悟り　心安らかに残照の余生を過ごしていた。
さりながら　思いがけなく室町殿の変事があり　配流の
われにも　赦免の沙汰があった。この島を青山の奥つ城と
思い定め　島の暮らしに慣れていたが　赦免も神意なれば
御心に従うまでと　すでに金春座を率いる婿殿も妻女も
住まう故郷の大和に帰るを思い立った。
手元が不如意なれば　一年ほど社の祭礼で神事の舞を奉じ

所望せる地頭殿に仕舞を教え　路銀を貯え　また婿殿の
援助も届き　ようやく支度を整え　名残を惜しむ国人に
別れを告げて　住み慣れたこの金島を離れ　付き人とともに
大和を指して旅立ったのだ。

八十路を越える老残の身に　長旅は難儀も多く　道中にて
倒れ伏すとも天命ならんと覚悟を定め　われを待ち侘びる
寿椿また娘と婿殿をただ安心させたい一念で　命がけで
旅を続けて　ようやく故郷の大和に帰り着いた。
賤が屋で家人と再会を喜んで間もなく　遂に老身は朽ち衰え
病床に臥した。やがて末期は近しと知りて　最後の禅定に入り
無心に出でたる真如の月を観ずれば　慈悲の光に照らされて
心は真に自在となった。かくていかに澄める心が　虚空の
大慈の光へ向けて引き上げられたか　今や別れの形見として
おんみに再現して見せよう。

　　　　旅の男

（傍白）おお　尊き天人が羽衣を大きく拡げ　透き通る身が
光を放ち　波打っている！　両手をゆっくり差し伸べて
静々と　草地を廻り始めた！

　　世阿弥の霊

禅定の無心は観じたり。近くは大和紀伊の山々　遠くは
瀬戸の潮路を谷間とし　西海へ広がる諸国　北国の果ての
海には遠く船路あり　遥か彼方の海上に　黄金の島も浮かび
見えたり。東北の国々は　山並遠く打ち続き　処々に雲を抜く
白衣の霊山の高嶺も見えたり。

景色は変じ　無礙（むげ）の慈光を浴びて　憩い静まる山野草木
なべて内より光を現し　わが身心をはぐくみ　無量光もて
世界を荘厳し　麗しきものを慕いて　高みに憧れ　わが行く
道を明かく照らせり。

心の鏡に映る海幸山幸　花果五穀　鳥獣家畜　ことごとく
人界先祖の生を養い　父母生み給いしわれを養い育て
過去現在の世の万象　一切の衆生が無辺の光を放ち
わが命を養いたるを観じたり。

十方世界の万象の慈悲の光は　いよいよ増して虚空に
広がり　たちまち押し寄せ　心を包み　解脱の心は
光明と化し　歓喜して　万象の光の天河とともに
無量光の本源に引き寄せられたり。光明を恋い慕う
心の光は　光明の源へ帰るなり　かくのごと。

旅の男

（独白）おお　天人の身がますます光り輝き　純白の天衣を
大きく羽ばたかせて　地面から舞い上がった！　羽衣を
ゆっくり揺らせて　白鷺のように旋回し舞い昇ってゆく！
何と神々しい舞だろう！　これこそ天上界の妙花の舞だ。
澄み昇る天花を出迎え　満天の星が降りてきてきらめいている。
上昇した天人は　星明かりの夜空に消えてしまった！

（ベンチに座っていた男は目を覚ます）

おや　いつの間にか眠りこんでいたらしい。
夜更けの草地で眠ったまま長い夢を見ていたのか。
夢の中で　この私が無意識に物語を作って　脳裏に
映したのか。それとも夢の中に　本当に天人が降りて
語ったのだろうか。
いずれにせよ　私が旅をして求めていた真の道を
夢幻のうちに暗示された気がする。今夜は
生涯忘れられない一夜になるだろう。
すでに月影は薄くなり　山際に傾いてしまい　残る星の
光も消えかかっている。東の空は曙色に染まり
夜が明けてきたらしい。
今日は　世阿弥の住んでいた泉の正法寺を訪れ　芸道の

聖を偲び　人生の先師を供養して冥福を祈ろう。

後書にかえて　作品の成立事情と主題

本書に収める二篇の内容と形式は奇異に感じられるかも知れない。それゆえ作品の解説を兼ねて、これらの成立事情と作者の意図した主題について記しておきたい。

三十代から私は舞台での演能を観劇し、能本を読んで能楽の世界に親しむようになった。その強烈な魅力は、詩と音楽と舞踊が渾然一体となって舞台上に表現する比類ない型の芸術美にあり、また能の簡勁な形式の奥深い表現力にあった。私は能の様式美をそなえる劇詩（上演を直接の目的としない劇的形式による詩作品）の創作を漠然と予感し、折に触れて着想した幾つかの素材をノートに書き留めておいた。

私が記しておいた劇詩の素材はノートの中に死蔵されたまま多年の歳月が経過した。だが思いがけない出来事が契機となって、埋もれていた素材の一つが芽を出した。三年前に宇宙史を主題とする詩集を刊行した直後に、私は大病を患い、手術を受けた。病床で私は病者の苦しみとキリストの十字架の受難を重ね合わせ、苦しみの秘義を黙想した。回復期に入ると、病室で書き留めた苦しみに関する断章を、ノートに眠っていたプロメテウス神話に結びつけ、作品にすることを思いついた。

この素材は次のような粗筋からなる前場・後場の二部構成による。コーカサスの山中で旅の修みた。

道士（ワキに相当）が土地の老人（前シテに相当）と出会い、小屋に案内される。老人は修道士をもてなし、山小屋で病苦に耐えつつ独り暮らしをしている身の上を打ち明け、周期的に襲う病苦に彼の病のための祈祷を加えるよう頼む。翌朝、修道士が山路を登ると、岩壁の炎の中に、縛られたプロメテウスの霊（後シテに相当）が出現する。驚いて問う修道士にプロメテウスは原始時代から現在に至るまで愛する人類の罪を償うために苦しみを受けていることを打ち明ける。修道士が祈るうちに、岩壁の炎が消えて、光る雲がプロメテウスの霊を包み天へ運び去る。

劇詩の制作に着手したとき、私は複式夢幻能の形式にとらわれているのに気づいた。人類に火と技術を伝えたために責め苦を受ける半神プロメテウスの神話は、人間精神の運命を象徴する物語として古代から哲学・文学の思想の対象となり、時代精神の変化とともに多様な解釈を生んできた。プロメテウス神話が内包する精神史的な含意、その思想の奥深さは、叙事形式の物語として解釈する必要があった。私は複式夢幻能の形式への固執から離れて、制作を進める過程で劇詩の素材を大きく変形した。

最初に意図した苦しみの主題が個人のレベルを超えて民族、さらに人類の苦しみにまで拡大されたために、前場の土地の老人を単なる病人ではなく、コーカサスやパレスチナの民の歴史を通じて戦争と平和について話す語り手とした。老人の病苦は、後に岩山の洞窟内で呻吟する老人の苦しみで表現し、その劇的効果を強めようと試

またプロメテウスのイメージを発展させて、人間精神の発達に助力する天使に変え、人類の罪の贖いのために苦しみを受ける天使に人類の心の歴史を語らせた。さらに人類の精神の運命と回心の必要を説き、苦しみの秘義と救いの道を告げ知らせる正義の天使を導入した。

その結果、登場人物が各々の立場から物語を展開する緩やかな構造をそなえる作品となった。劇詩の様式が、人間の意志と行為の現在を表現する劇的要素の外に、事象の展開を客観的に物語る叙事的要素、個人的体験の感動を主観的に表出する抒情的要素の併存を可能にし、表現するべき思想感情の拡大と複数の声の導入を可能にする柔軟で寛容な形式になり得ることを、この制作の体験によって私は知った。

劇詩の可能性を信じて、私は引き続き同じ形式の作品を構想した。「世阿弥」の素材も複式夢幻能の形式を模したものであった。この形式において前場のシテは普通の人、現世の人であり、彼の生の現状を表現する。後場のシテは鬼神、天人、死霊、精霊などの類いで、霊的な存在らしく言葉と象徴的な身振りによって自在に時空を超え、生前の過去を再現して見せたり、霊界での状態を現在化して見せたりする。このような構成の強烈な対比が、観客を目的として見られる舞台上の複式夢幻能の劇的効果を強めている。上演を目的としない劇詩を制作する過程で、その形式の劇的な対比は殆ど失われたが、基本構造を失わずに、前後の場の登場人物が各々の立場と視点で語りを展開する作品となった。

夢幻能は、文芸の視点から見れば夢物語の形式をそなえる。夢は、戯曲、抒情詩、叙事文芸など主要な文芸様式に広く使える表現方法である。近現代の文芸は、夢の領域を拡大して、怪奇と恐怖を表現する悪夢、日常の生を離れ超現実の世界を探る幻想、夢幻の雰囲気を醸し出す夢想など、多様な夢を展開させている。概して近現代の文芸に表れる夢は、感覚的な意識野に彷徨する夢で、近現代の文学精神が感覚野を偏重してきた状況を証明するものであろう。古代人が尊重した夢の神託の名残ともいうべき無意識から生じる夢の警告の機能を文芸の表現に利用する場合もあるが、それは最早文芸における夢の重要な技法ではない。

しかし芸術に昇華し生に秩序を与える夢には、倫理性や宗教性が内在していて、精神生活の未来へ向けて働く夢の機能をもっと重視したい。中世ヨーロッパの宗教詩は、作者と聴衆・読者を理想の地上の楽園、さらには天上界の光明に導く超現実の時空として高い夢を想像し、詩の言葉に表現した。作中の夢見る人は、夢の最後に究極の光景を垣間見て目覚め、大いなる慰めと希望を得て現世を生きてゆく。この状態の夢を求める想像力は、メタノイア（心境変化・回心）の動態を示している。一方、近現代の文芸に多く見られる低い夢を求める想像力は、メタモルフォーシス（形態変化・魔術的変身）の動態を示して本質を変えることなく幻想を限りなく変転させる。

私はメタノイア型の想像力による詩を求め、文芸における高い夢

の可能性を信じて作品に造形することを試みた。この理想的な夢の技法を用いることによって本書の二篇に共通する物語の筋（プロット）と構造形式が確保された。両方とも求道の旅人が途上で夢幻を体験し、霊的存在が語って示した人生の知恵と真理を学び知って旅を続けるという物語の構造をそなえている。前の作品では、夢幻の中で天使が人間精神の進むべき正道を示し、後の作品では、夢の中で天人が悟りへの道を示す。前者はキリスト教思想を背景とし、後者は仏教思想、特に禅思想を背景としているので、異なる宗教の精神世界を表現しているように見えるが、苦悩する人間の救済という根本の主題において二篇は共通している。前者では、人間が個人のレベルでも民族・人類のレベルでも回心と神の信仰によって救われることを語り、後者では、人間が回心と悟りを求める修行によって救われることを語っている。佐渡へ流された後の世阿弥の消息は、伝存する小謡曲舞集の「金島書」と金春大夫（禅竹）宛書状一通によって窺い知るだけで、その終焉の地も没年も不明で世阿弥晩年の実像は謎に包まれている。私は、神仏に帰依し、悟りを求め続けて救われる人間を想像して描いた。

前の作品では、天使が苦しみの秘義を説き、苦しみと死の過ぎ越しによる新生を告げる。後の作品では、天人が苦しみを超克する禅定による解脱を語る。宗教の教理、言語、制度などに相違があっても、宗教的精神の超越作用、宗教的実存の超越志向は、すべての宗教に共通している。宗教体験を生きる実存は、神あるいは絶対者を求め超越して止まない。キリストを求める修道者の道と悟りを求める仏道修行者の道は通じ合う道であろう。宗教間の対話と相互理解の時代を生きる文学の精神は、このような宗教的実存の普遍の道に光を当てようとする。私の劇詩二篇も、その道を照明する試みだったと思う。

さらに、これらの作品は人間と自然界の深い関わりを暗示している。人間の癒しと救済に示される超自然の恩恵である自然界の恩恵が副主題として、二篇の前場・後場に通底して響き合っていることに読者は気づくであろう。それぞれの場で、豊かな自然環境が人間の身心と生命を支え、自然の恩恵を受けて生の充実が可能になることを暗示している。前の作品の後場では、この問題を掘り下げ、共に病んだ自然界と人間の実相を表現し、両者の癒しと救済のヴィジョンを示した。なお、後の作品では、芸術を求道とする芸術家の在り方という問題を新たに提起しているが、芸術を求道とする芸術観によって考察している以上、これは主題に従属する副主題とみなすべきである。

上述のように概観すれば、二篇が大筋において共通の形式と主題によって連関する作品として形を成したのは明らかで、それゆえこの二篇を連作として本書に収めた。

これらの作品の制作に当たっても、多くの文献資料を必要とした。前の作品では、旧新約聖書を初め、神学・哲学・史学・人類学の領域の研究書、さらにコーカサス地方に関する地誌・研究書・論文から多くの知識と情報を得ている。後の作品では、仏教の経典・禅語

録・法話を初め、世阿弥の謡曲・伝書（能楽論・芸談・他）及び世阿弥に関する研究書に拠った外、古語については、中古・中世の和歌・物語・随筆などを適宜参照するとともに、種々の古語辞典、特に『時代別国語大辞典・室町時代編一―五』（三省堂、一九八五―二〇〇一）を活用した。作品中の方言については、佐渡方言の貴重な辞典であり研究書でもある廣田貞吉『佐渡方言辞典』（自家版、昭和四十九年）を活用することができた。

　新しい芸術表現は、作者が時間をかけて蓄えた精神文化の伝統、心に内蔵した芸術、宗教、哲学思想などの生きている伝統に作者の心が働きかけて生み出された新しい精神的生命である。芸術の制作と表現は、懐胎と出産に喩えられる。作者は自己を滅却し、無の状態にして内なる精神の伝統との交わりを深め、新しい客観的精神を生み出す。この新しい生命は独立し、精神の共同体に参加して、芸術の立場から人間精神の進展にわずかでも貢献しようとする。

　それゆえ作品は、作者を離れ、精神世界の未来へ向けて旅立つ。このささやかな二篇が未知の読者の魂に伝わり、共感と生への真の希望を与えることができれば幸いである。

　最後に、この小著の刊行に当たって、助言を頂き、さらに解説文を書いて頂いたコールサック社の鈴木比佐雄氏に心から感謝したい。併せて、本書の完成に尽力されたスタッフの方々に厚くお礼を申し上げる。

二〇一七年六月

守口　三郎

守口三郎（もりぐち　さぶろう）略歴

一九三五年　東京市滝野川区田端町（現・北区田端）に生まれる
一九四二年　千代田区内神田区立神龍小学校に入学
一九四四年　疎開により福岡県遠賀郡水巻町に転居
一九五九年　九州大学文学部文学科（英語学英文学専攻）卒業
一九六二年　同大学院文学研究科（英文学専攻）修士課程修了
一九六二─六七年　高知女子大学文学部、一九六七─八四年　佐賀大学教育学部、
一九八四─二〇〇一年　愛媛大学法文学部・大学院法文学研究科で英語英文学の教育研究に従事
一九七九─八〇年　英国ケンブリッジ大学で英文学研究に従事
二〇〇一年　定年退職
二〇〇二年　京都府精華町に転居、国会図書館関西館所蔵の文献資料を利用し研究執筆活動を続ける
二〇一九年六月三日　逝去

専門分野及び研究テーマ

英文学
　　近代英詩の実存論的研究　　　　　　　　　　　　　（一九六〇─七五年）
　　ルネサンス初期英詩の研究─変動期の詩の実験　　　（一九七六─八一年）
　　イェイツの文学理念の形成と近代批判　　　　　　　（一九八二─八八年）

西洋文学
　　西洋文学における病と癒しの精神史的考察　　　　　（一九八九─二〇〇〇年）

詩学
　　詩的想像力による科学的宇宙像変容の研究　　　　　（二〇〇二─一四年）

詩歴　詩学研究の傍ら一九五九年より作詩、一九八七年より作歌を試みる

著書

歌集『山径集』　　　　　　　　　砂子屋書房　　一九九二年

エッセイ『西欧芸術への旅』　　　ＮＣＩ　　　　一九九五年

評論『病と文学』　　　　　　　　英宝社　　　　二〇〇〇年

詩集『魂の宇宙』　　　　　　　　コールサック社　二〇一四年

詩集『劇詩　受難の天使　世阿弥』コールサック社　二〇一七年

英日詩集『劇詩　受難の天使　世阿弥』コールサック社　二〇二〇年

解説　夢幻能を駆使した劇詩の可能性

――守口三郎『劇詩　受難の天使　世阿弥』に寄せて

鈴木比佐雄

1

守口三郎さんは、一九三五年に東京に生まれ、九州大学大学院文学研究科で英文学、詩学を修めた後に高知・佐賀・愛媛の大学で教鞭をとり、退職後の現在は京都に暮らしている。一九九二年に歌集『山径集』、一九九五年にイギリスをはじめとする西欧の国々の絵画、演劇などの芸術との内的な対話を記した紀行文『西欧芸術への旅』、二〇〇年に刊行したソポクレースの詩劇などの西欧の古典から「病と癒し」をテーマとした評論集『病と文学』を刊行した。そして二〇一四年に第一詩集『魂の宇宙』を刊行した。その詩集の解説で私は次のように紹介した。

守口三郎さんの詩の特長は、「叡智の心臓」というような言葉でも明らかなように、観念と物質が融合された表現がされていて、さらにその心臓の心室から「脈搏つ時空」が迸り出てくる瞬間を感じている。頭脳でもある心臓から新たな時空が誕生することを賛美しているかのようだ。その意味では、守口さんは自己の身体に宇宙の誕生を感受することを原点にしてこの詩篇を開始したことが分かる。（略）さらに「叡智を宇宙に映す聖なる意志よ」や最終行の「万象の宇宙を擁する主の意志へ向け　飛翔するのか」と言った創造主の存在を守口さんは強く意識していることが理解されてくる。賢治が法華経に帰依していたように、守口さんも敬虔な宗教心を抱いていて、宇宙の発端から終末まで「主の意志」を見いだしてしまったのかも知れない。科学と宗教心が対話しながらこれらの詩篇が生み出されていった。

〈「銀河を包む透明な意志」を展開する人〉より

守口さんは、そのような宇宙の誕生から終末に至るまでの宇宙の存在の響きを「主の意志」として聴き取ってしまい、それを「魂の宇宙」として情熱的に書き記してしまった。

ところが出版後にかつて研究者として滞在していたヨーロッパを再訪されると聞いていたが、検査で内臓の疾患が発見されて緊急手術をすることになった。その手術は成功し数か月後にお見舞いの電話で話した際に、私は本当に驚かされた。生死を賭けた術後の静養中に次の詩集の構想を抱いてメモをしていることを、いつもの物静かな口調でしかも情熱的に語られていたからだ。私は守口さんがこの大病によって何か想像を超えた「聖なる意志」を確認しえたのかも知れないと感じた。その時の構想をじっくりと二年数か月をかけて守口さんは今回の『劇詩　受難の天使　世阿弥』として誕生させたのだった。

新詩集は二つの劇詩『受難の天使』、『世阿弥』と「後書にかえて　作品の成立事情と主題」から成り立っている。

まず『受難の天使』を読んでみて私は、日本の詩人がこのような十二世紀末の南コーカサス山中を舞台とした、四人の登場人物である「旅の修道士」と「土地の老人」と二人の天使たちとの迫真の劇詩を書きえたことが、何か奇跡のようにも感じられた。しかし二番目の劇詩『世阿弥』と「後書にかえて　作品の成立事情と主題」を読み、鑑賞を繰り返していた世阿弥の「複式夢幻能」の形式が潜在的に手助けをしていたことや、また西欧での観劇の経験から演劇的な要素を入れて、展開することによってその精神性が劇的に表現されたことを理解できた。

2

受難の天使』は第一場から第五場に分かれている。第一場「峠へ通じる山路」、第二場「谷間の小屋」、第三場「山頂近くの小路」は、能の「前場（まえば）」に当たり、現実の「土地の老人」（主人公の前シテ）と「旅の修道士」（脇役のワキ）の出会い、その一期一会の交流が互いの生き方を思索的な言葉に込めて無理なく描かれている。守口さんが短歌をされていたことも七五調の韻律を効果的に台詞や「傍白」に込められている。第四場「岩場の洞窟」、第五場「岩山の路傍」は、能の「後場（のちば）」に該当するのだろう。第四場「岩場の洞窟」で「土地の老人」は病苦に苛まれ、人類に火を教えた

罪を背負った「プロメテウス」に成り代わって、人類の苦しみを抱えて悶え苦しむのだ。第五場「岩場の路傍」はさらに「プロメテウス」から人類の罪を贖う「助力の天使」にその罪を辛辣に語らせて、その果てに「正義の天使」らの「後シテ」によって人類の救済の可能性を告げさせる。それを見届けて「旅の修道士」は次のように語る。

今こそ私は知る。この岩山が私の聖地となったのを。
聖地は名高い巡礼の地に限らない。聖地は至る所にあるのだ。
神が人の心を訪れるとき　心が聖地となるからだ。
私の心の聖地が悪に汚されず　変わらぬ聖所であり続けますように。

聖地エルサレムを目指していた「旅の修道士」は、「聖地は至る所にある」と悟り、次の「聖地」である修道院に向かい、聖地エルサレムを目指すのだ。

守口さんには霊感ともいえる「助力の天使」や「正義の天使」が降りてきてしまって、人類の様々な罪を語り、その罪を救済するための回心の仕方をも語らせている。と同時に「旅の修道士」も「土地の老人」も主役脇役を超えて、あたかも天使の受難を引き受けるかのような精神の在り方によって、私たちを精神の高みに同伴させてくれる。この劇詩を読み終えると魅力的な文体から心に「聖なるもの」が満ちてくる思いがしてくる。

次の劇詩『世阿弥』は、長年親しんできた「複式夢幻能」を完成させた世阿弥に感謝し、その世阿弥の想像力の源に守口さんは肉薄し、世阿弥を甦らせて本人にその芸術精神を語らせようと試みたのだろう。『世阿弥』は、第一場「七浦海岸」、第二場「佐和田の松林　テントの中」、第三場「松林の空き地」から成っている。第一場「七浦海岸」は、「前場」に当たり、佐渡の七浦海岸を訪れた「旅の男」（ワキ）、「土地の老人」（前シテ）との出会いと互いの身の上話から始まり親密感が増したところで別れとなる。第二場「佐和田の松林　テントの中」では、「旅の男」がキャンプ場で、

「昔流人の法師が庵を結んでいた」ことを想起し、「林で摘んだ一輪の野菊を活けこの小皿を香炉として　一抹の香を焚こう」とし、さらに「清らかな湯で茶を点てて法師の霊に一碗を捧げよう」とした。第三場の「後場」につなげるためにこの第二場は必要だったのだろう。第三場「松林の空き地」では、「世阿弥の霊」が「天の光明界」より「手向けの香花」と「茶湯の香り」に誘われて、かつて自らが流された島の松林に舞い降りてくる。「世阿弥の霊」は、「旅の男」の問いに答えて、武家政治に翻弄され辛酸をなめたが、それでも芸の道を究めていった人生を回想し、その時の思いを語り始める。守口さんは「世阿弥の霊」に乗り移るために「複式夢幻能」の形式とそれを生み出した本人に物語らせるという驚くべき手法でそれを劇詩に刻んだ。「世阿弥の霊」が松林で舞いながら能について語ったせりふは次のように締めくくられている。

厳冬の下界静まる極寒の夜　物を離れ　人を離れ　我を
離れて　雪の明かりの凍原に立ち　冴えまさる銀河を仰ぎ
ほのかに瞬く群星の声明（しょうみょう）を謡に　天界の妙なる調べを音曲に
黙照の天の広座に進み出で　　妙境現成（げんじょう）　光明歓喜の舞を奉じた。

このように守口さんの劇詩『受難の天使』と劇詩『世阿弥』は、私たちが忘れかけていた中世の生み出した芸術・宗教が現代につながる豊かな精神性を新たにして伝えてくれる。これらの守口さんの劇詩が、声の通る小さな劇場で静かに演じられて、キリスト教と禅の思想の真髄が世阿弥の「複式夢幻能」の形式によって多くの人びとに再び宿っていくことを願っている。

（解説は日本語のみ収録）

訳者の序文

この本「劇詩　受難の天使・世阿弥」を最初読んだとき、わたしは著者の多くの分野における深遠な知識と優れた文学的才能に深い感銘を受けた。著者守口三郎教授は旧約聖書、新約聖書、神学、哲学、歴史、人類学、地理に関する書籍に加えて、コーカサス地方の研究も参考にされたという。二番目の劇詩「世阿弥」に関しては、広く仏教の経典、禅語録、法話、能、世阿弥の伝書、世阿弥に関する研究書を参考にされたという。著者はまた「時代別国語大辞典・室町時代編」「佐渡方言辞典」も参考にされた。

最初の劇詩の第五場で援助の天使は、人間の樹上生活から、両足で歩く地上生活への進化と人間の飽く事を知らない貪欲によって引き起こされている深刻な問題が、次のような文章で述べられている。

「人々は農耕や牧畜の技術を身につけた　こうして生活はより安定し　子孫を増やした。だが生存の本能を超え自己保存の意識を強めた人類は　欲望が募り　遂にうねり渦巻く欲望の泥海から　魔性の我欲の毒蛇が躍り出たのだ……」

「物を必要以上に所有し貯えると　他の部族の侵略を恐れ　防塁を作り武装した。恐怖は不信を生み　不信は敵意を生み　敵意は攻撃を誘発した　恐怖は悪心の母胎なのだ……」

それから、正義の天使が言う。

「朝日を浴びる人々は　冷えた化石の心を温かい血肉の心に
変えられる。かれらは滅びの車を降りて　夜明けの世界の
大地を踏みしめ　その感覚を取り戻し　ゆっくり歩き出す。

かれらは立ち止まり　大地の傷を涙と汗で癒し　大地の病を
同情と労苦で治す。荒地を緑野に変え　甦った草花を愛で
戻ってきた鳥の歌を聴き　大地の恵みの実りを収める」

この劇詩「受難の天使」はすごく鮮やかに、力強く、美しく、書かれていて、今までに書かれた最も重要な劇詩の
一篇である、とわたしは思う。

二番目の劇詩「世阿弥」は佐渡を旅行している失職中の現代日本人男性と能役者、能劇作者、批評家、世阿弥（一三六三
―一四四三）の霊との対話が主体となっている。第三場で世阿弥の霊は旅行者にこう言っている。

「春麗らかな一日は　　海辺に行きて　白波寄せる荒磯に立ち
魚群れる早潮望み　　轟き響む海鳴りを　龍神うなる謡とし
岩壁を打つ怒濤を鼓に　海の涯より照り渡る光に向かい
鰭魚恵む神仏に　　沖の漁りの無事祈り　風を鎮める舞を捧げた」

「遠山に　花の雲の霞かかれば　花に誘われ　心浮き
急ぎ出で立ち　山路分け入り　風に散り舞う花の光に
万象の心を観じ　野辺に咲き散りゆく花を惜しめども

心より心に映る面影の光の花こそ　常住不滅の花と知り
われは空の桜の精となり　山渡り花吹き散らす嵐を笛に
行方を知らず　無常安穏　転身歓喜　仏法散華の舞を踊った」

「行く春を惜しみ送るも　今は限りと心がけ　風薫り
花咲きすさぶ野にも出で　色とりどりの花と語らい
光さす青葉若葉の林に入れば　ほしいまま鳴く山鳥を
笛と鼓に　谷川の高鳴る音を謡とし　精爽やかな社で舞い
風そよぐ植田に立ちて　黄金の瑞穂の実りを祈り　遠田の
蛙の天にも届く声を謡に　望み見る満目青山を讃えて舞った」

この序文で、わたしがどんな言葉を使っても守口三郎教授のこの劇詩の美しさ、力強さ、素晴らしさ、を十分に説明することは出来ない。作品そのものに説明してもらいましょう。この素晴らしい二篇の劇詩を英訳することは、わたしにとって実に素晴らしい経験でした。世界中の読者が、老いも若きもこの本を愛読してくれることを期待しています。この英訳書を海外の読者も対象にして出版するに当たり大きな援助を下さった守口三郎教授夫人とコールサック社代表鈴木比佐雄氏に深い感謝を述べたい。この英訳書を編集して下さった清泉大学のブルース・アレン教授にも心から感謝申し上げたい。そして世阿弥に関する質問に答えてくれた相模原市立図書館の館員の方々にも深く感謝いたします。最後に、文体に関して、いくつかの名詞、形容詞の重要性を強調する目的で、その頭文字を、わたしの判断で大文字にしたことを読者の皆さんにご了解頂きたい、と思います。例えば

"Fear bred Distrust, Distrust bred Hostility,
Hostility induced Attacks. Fear is the Mother of Wickedness…"

恐怖は不信を生み、不信は敵意を生み
敵意は攻撃を誘発した　恐怖は悪心の母胎なのだ……

注・恐怖 (fear)、不信 (distrust)、敵意 (hostility)、攻撃 (attack) など抽象名詞は、文中に出てくるときは小文字で始まる
のが普通であるが、意味を強める目的で頭文字を大文字にした

詩人・東洋大学名誉教授
二〇一九年十一月

郡山　直